" *These are marvelous stories where all elements including descriptions of settings, characters and plot are done to perfection. The author has followed the approaches of the original Doyle stories to the extent that these could have been easily included in the original works. The biggest disappointment to my mind was realizing when the book was running out of pages. I hope this author has more in the works. I can hardly wait.*"

" *Mr. Ashton is simply the best current writer of the Holmes pastiche. In reviews of his previous works, I have noted the purity of his classic language as if from the pen of Conan Doyle 100 years ago. While there are many many Holmes stories on the market, Hugh has the unique ability to channel ACD and Dr. Watson to come up with new stories that satisfy the longing of any Sherlockian purist for more original stories.*"

" *Mr. Ashton has mined another group of enjoyable Sherlock Holmes stories in the treasure trove of material mysteriously passed to him by Dr. Watson. If you are a fan of Holmes and Watson you will enjoy these new tales. This book is the latest in Mr. Ashton's series of excellent pastiches, that appear to be right out of the Canon.*"

Mr. Sherlock Holmes – Notes on some Singular Cases
: Five Untold Adventures of Sherlock Holmes
Hugh Ashton

ISBN-13: 978-1-912605-34-7
ISBN-10: 1-91-260534-1
Published by j-views Publishing, 2018
© 2017, 2018 Hugh Ashton & j-views Publishing

The adventure of " John Vincent Harden" first appeared in *The MX Book of New Sherlock Holmes Stories - Part IV*, and that of the " Deceased Doctor" in *The MX Book of New Sherlock Holmes Stories - Part V*.

This is a work of fiction. Names, characters, places, brands, media, and incidents are either the product of the author's imagination or are written in respectful tribute to the creator of the principal characters.

Mr. Sherlock Holmes – Notes on Some Singular Cases

CONTENTS

PREFACE

T has been some time since I have had the leisure to examine the notes left by Doctor Watson regarding the cases in which he was involved with his famous friend, Sherlock Holmes.

I confess that I had considered the well of stories to be almost dry, which in part accounted for my reluctance to continue. However, I was delighted that in addition to the two adventures which have recently appeared in the anthologies recently compiled by David Marcum: that of John Vincent Harden, and of the Deceased Doctor, two more, both referenced in the Canon and worthy of inclusion, also surfaced.

The Adventure of the Deceased Doctor shows a Holmes and Watson following the events of His Last Bow, at a time when the spirit of England was almost at its lowest. It is gratifying to see, though, how the friendship between these two remarkable men (and I truly believe Watson to be as remarkable in his way as his more famous friend) survived the rigours and horrors of the Great War.

The other adventures take place in the "classical" or Canonical period, which is probably more familiar to most readers.

In any event, these discoveries have given me new hope that there are still further adventures to be edited and presented to the world.

Hugh Ashton
Lichfield and Kamakura
April 2017

MR. SHERLOCK HOLMES – NOTES ON SOME SINGULAR CASES

DISCOVERED AND EDITED BY

HUGH ASHTON

J-VIEWS PUBLISHING, LICHFIELD, ENGLAND

THE ADVENTURE OF THE BROKEN DOOR

HAVE had occasion to remark that on many occasions, the views of Sherlock Holmes with regard to the law and justice were not those that would meet with the approval of our lawyers or judges. Despite his expertise in the detection of crime, he hardly ever appeared in court as a witness for the prosecution in the cases which he had brought to a successful conclusion.

" My business is not to convict the criminals," he explained to me once, when I upbraided him regarding his release of certain individuals who were, beyond all possible doubt, guilty of the crimes that Holmes was investigating, " but rather, to determine the facts of the case, and to lay them before those whose job it is to perform the legal niceties, should, in my opinion, the occasion and circumstances demand it."

My personal view, which I did not express to him, was that Holmes cared little for the morality or otherwise of the cases on which he was engaged, preferring simply the mental challenge of the chase. In the vast majority of cases, however, the views of Holmes and those of the guardians of the law eventually coincided, and the events described here form one of these.

I was scanning the *Morning Post* one spring day, and Holmes was poring over the agony columns in the previous day's *Times* in an attempt to discover a problem worthy of his talents. It had been a particularly uneventful month up to the time I am describing, and Holmes had been engaged in a series of malodorous chemical experiments, the results of which continued to permeate the air. Our long-suffering landlady, Mrs. Hudson, had made no verbal comment when she entered our rooms that morning, but her look of injured innocence would have penetrated the heart of a man more stony-hearted than Holmes, and he had been forced to mutter some sort of apology to her.

" See here, Holmes !" I exclaimed. " ' Family of four found

slain in Bermondsey'. According to this report, Inspector Lestrade has been assigned to the case, but at present has few ideas as to how the unfortunates might have met their ends, other than that they were assaulted by a person or persons unknown with a blunt instrument, which is still undiscovered."

" Somewhat unlike Lestrade," remarked Holmes. " He has usually formulated a theory within the first thirty minutes of being assigned to a case, regardless of whether or not it matches the facts as they present themselves. Invariably, the theory turns out to be incorrect, and when he does catch his man, it is almost always a matter more of luck than judgement."

" Surely you must credit him with some qualities ?" I enquired. Lestrade had worked with Holmes on many cases in the past, and it pained me a little to hear one who had become almost a friend to be denigrated in such a fashion.

" Why yes," Holmes answered me. " He is brave, tenacious, and possessed of an iron will. Though I do not rate his mental faculties at all highly, there is no-one – with one notable exception – that I would sooner have by my side in times of trouble. Furthermore, like you, Watson, he possesses the invaluable gift of silence on many occasions."

" I am glad that you find it possible to credit him with some qualities," I laughed.

" Oh, he has his qualities, all right," smiled Holmes. " Tell me more about this Bermondsey murder."

" It says here that the bodies were discovered yesterday evening by a friend, a Mr. George Timmins, who had called on the husband, Albert Stevens. Timmins knocked on the door, but on receiving no answer, entered the house. Stevens was not at home, but on entering the house, Timmins stumbled over the bodies of the wife, Mary, the two daughters, Elizabeth and Jane, and the youngest child, George. All had been brutally beaten about the head and shoulders. Indeed, the wife's face had been so battered that her identity could only be confirmed by the rings on her fingers."

" What age were the girls ?"

" Elizabeth's age is given as nineteen, and that of Jane as sixteen. The son, George, was twelve years old."

" And the address where all this took place ?"

" In Bermondsey, as I remarked earlier. Webster Street is given as the address."

" Indeed ?" he replied. " In the agony column here is a message written in an elementary cypher, which reads, " To GT, meet me at the railway end of Webster Street at three this afternoon. All love and godspeed, MS.' There, what do you make of that, eh ?"

" It is an interesting coincidence, I agree. The name of the street—"

" And the initials, man ! MS. Mary Stevens, or I am a Dutchman."

I shook my head. " You are too much, Holmes. Why, they could be Michael or Mark Smith, and there are any number of streets by that name in London alone."

" To the best of my memory, there is a Webster Crescent and a Webster Gardens in London, but only one Webster Street. Furthermore, that street in Bermondsey runs down towards the railway," answered my friend. " You are well aware of my little hobby, that of possessing a knowledge of the streets and squares of the metropolis, are you not ?"

" It still seems to be something of a coincidence," I said to Holmes.

" What appears to the untrained eye to be merely coincidence," he told me, " to the trained observer is often a vital link in the chain of reasoning."

I found myself unable to answer this. " In any event, I am certain that we will discover more," I said. " If Lestrade is at a loss, these rooms are usually his first port of call."

In the event, however, it was not Inspector Lestrade who was responsible for a more direct introduction to the " Bermondsey Tragedy", as the newspapers had it. The day following the conversation recorded above, Mrs. Hudson announced a client, and a somewhat diffident young man was shown into the room.

" Mr. Holmes," he said to my friend, in a voice which seemed hardly louder than that of a small child, " you must help me, or I am a dead man."

I had taken in the details of our visitor's dress, and following the principles that I had learned from Sherlock Holmes, deduced from his ink-stained fingers that he was a clerk. Though his clothing had once been of good quality, it had obviously been cut for a different man, and the cuffs and hems were showing distinct signs of wear. The hat, though again of good quality, was of an older style, and had likewise seen better days. As for the man himself, he appeared timid in the extreme. His eyes failed to meet those of either Holmes or myself, and darted about the room in a nervous fashion, as if expecting a sudden assault from an unexpected quarter.

" Indeed ?" enquired Holmes calmly. " And from what quarter do you expect this danger to come ?"

" From the courts, Mr. Holmes. From the police," were his astonishing words. Holmes said nothing in reply, but merely raised an eyebrow.

" Have you heard of the deaths at Bermondsey ?" continued our visitor. Holmes nodded. " The police will come for me. They believe I killed them, but I swear that I am innocent of any crime. For the love of God, Mr. Holmes, you must assist me, no matter what the cost."

" I will hear your story first, and then decide whether I am to render you the assistance you seek," Holmes replied. " Watson, if you will please do your duty ?"

I recognised this as Holmes' usual command for me to sit

attentively with notebook and pencil, and record our visitor's account.

" My name," he began, " is Albert Stevens and I am twenty-three years old. I am employed as a clerk by Richardson & Co., Ltd. of Warren Street. They are agents who provide insurance for importers of various goods from overseas, and I have been with them for the past three years. I am married— forgive me." Here he buried his face in his hands and appeared to be sobbing. I half-rose, as if to make for the brandy decanter, but Holmes stopped me with a wave of his hand. Surprised at this somewhat cavalier attitude to another's distress, I nonetheless sat silently until the fit had passed. At length, Stevens sat up, and dabbed at his eyes with a somewhat less than clean handkerchief.

" Forgive me," he repeated. " I was about to say that I am married, but the realisation that I must now use the past tense struck me hard, and I was overcome. I was married to Mary Stevens, until her death that you have seen reported in the newspapers."

" A question, Mr. Stevens, if I may. As well as Mary Stevens, the deaths of three of her children were reported, the age of the eldest being given as nineteen. You have just informed us that you are all of twenty-three years old. Perhaps you would care to elucidate ?"

This brought a wry half-smile to the lips of the other. " Indeed, that is the case. My marriage to Mary was not her first such. We met about a year ago through the offices of a mutual friend. Her previous husband had passed away some months previously, and we formed a friendship which ripened. I had misgivings, I admit, regarding an alliance with a woman, the age of whose eldest child was closer to my age than was hers, but she assured me that there would be no problem in that regard, and indeed, there was none."

" I see," said Holmes. " Proceed, if you would."

" I have no alibi for my whereabouts at the time that their death is assumed to have occurred, other than my own word, and I fear that without the assistance of someone such as yourself, Mr. Holmes, it will go hard with me if the police should accuse me of these hideous crimes."

" What reason would they have to suspect you rather than another ?"

" Are not most murders committed by members of the household ? Surely the laws of probability, if nothing else, would lead me to be suspected ?"

" There is something in what you say. You also say ' if nothing else'. There is more ?"

The other sighed. " I fear so. Who else would have a key to the house, allowing them to enter, perform the dastardly deed, and then lock the door behind them ? The door of the house had to be broken down by Mr. George Timmins, my neighbour, as I think has been reported in the newspapers."

" That would indeed appear to be a mark against you," commented Holmes. " Pray, tell me where you were when these deaths are said to have occurred ?"

" I was on an errand from the office in Warren Street to one of our clients in Southwark."

" The client's name ?"

" Lightfoot & Sons, importers of machinery from the United States. Their address is 21 Lafone Street."

" Then someone at that address would be able to vouch for your movements ?" I enquired.

He seemed to brighten visibly at my suggestion. " Why, yes, of course. They would. I do not know how I did not come to consider that earlier."

Holmes appeared to be on the verge of speaking, but I observed him check himself, and once more relax into that characteristic position of his, eyes half-closed, and fingertips pressed together, almost as if in prayer.

" So you will take my case, Mr. Holmes ?" implored our visitor.

" I do not consider that you have a case at present, Mr. Stevens," replied Sherlock Holmes. " In the event, however, that the police do take you up, you may tell them that you have consulted me. I am well-known at Scotland Yard, and they will pass on the information to me."

" Why, thank you, Mr. Holmes. And as to your fee... ?"

Holmes smiled. " Let us cross that bridge when we come to it, shall we ? I can assure you that should your case require a fee, you will not find it to be excessive."

" That is at least one thing I may smile about," answered Stevens. " Though God knows there is little enough of that."

With that, he bade us farewell and left us.

" Well, Watson, what do you make of him ?"

" He rang false, but I cannot put my finger on why I consider that to be the case."

" Excellent. I believe we do indeed have a false coin here. What did you make of his profession ?"

" He told us, did he not, that he worked as a clerk in an insurance company ? And he certainly displayed the ink stains I would associate with that profession."

" But not the tell-tale creases in the sleeves, nor the hunched posture typical of those who would describe themselves as clerks," objected Holmes. " In any event, the clothes he was wearing were not his own, I will take my oath on that."

" They might have been mourning clothes, and therefore borrowed or hired," I pointed out.

" Indeed they might have been," he agreed. " But I do not think that they were. I do not think our Mr. Stevens is as heartbroken at his loss as he might seem to be. And there is one other matter."

" The forgotten alibi ?"

" Precisely, Watson. A man comes to me, seemingly in

terror that he shall be hanged for a crime he claims he did not commit, begging me to find the evidence that shall set him free, when all the time, the alibi is there."

" He has an innocent face," I pointed out, " and he may well be out of his depth with these events which have caused his life to take such a sudden turn for the worse. Indeed, he reminded me of nothing so much as one of those innocent missionaries to the poor, or Sunday-school teachers, who are so unworldly that when confronted with the evils of this world, lose all comprehension and their wits temporarily desert them. He may be confused and have genuinely overlooked the fact that he has a witness as to his innocence."

" It is possible, once more, that you are correct," said Holmes. " However, it does not seem at all likely to me that this is the case, despite his Sunday-school appearance. I fear we are moving in deep waters here and must proceed with an appropriate degree of caution."

" Will you take his case if he is arrested ?"

" I will look into the case even if he is not," replied Holmes smartly. " Come, let us pay a visit to Lestrade at Scotland Yard."

It was some thirty minutes later that we found ourselves facing the police agent across his desk. Despite Holmes' denigrating comments, I had always found Lestrade to be not unintelligent, even if not the most astute of observers, and his tenacity and courage were beyond dispute.

Holmes related the facts relating to our earlier visitor, and Lestrade nodded.

" Well, there's no denying that he's right when it comes to members of the family being the first ones we suspect in cases like this. But I have to tell you that there's more to this one than meets the eye. We'd been keeping something of a watch on that Mary Stevens, or Mary Holt, as she was before she made this last marriage."

" Indeed ? " Holmes queried politely.

" We had her down as a fence – a receiver of stolen goods. Those girls of hers – no better than they should be, believe me. The young lad – well, he's young, but they're never too young to get into trouble, eh, Mr. Holmes ? "

" True, " Holmes agreed.

" Now whether your precious Sunday-school teacher is aware of these things or not, of course we have no idea, " Lestrade continued. " Naturally we questioned him when the crime was first discovered, but he appeared to be too overcome with emotion to make any rational response to our questions. "

" He never mentioned the fact that he had been questioned by your men, " I said, surprised at Lestrade's words.

" What of the man who discovered the bodies ? This neighbour, Timmins ? " asked Holmes.

" Neighbour ? " answered Lestrade in some surprise. " George Timmins is a native of Blackheath. No neighbour of your Mr. Stevens, and I doubt that he was a friend of his, either. He's another one we've had our eye on for some time. He got six months two years ago for housebreaking, and I'd lay odds that he's still at the same game, but he's a crafty one, and so far we've failed to get the goods on him. "

" And did he have business dealings, shall we say, with the late Mrs. Stevens ? "

" Again, we have no proof, but I would be surprised if that were not the case. We had nothing out of him when we picked him up after he discovered the bodies, and we had to let him loose. "

" One matter puzzles me, " said Holmes. " According to the newspaper reports, this Timmins was coming to visit at least one of the Stevens family. How does he come to explain the fact that he broke down the door ? Surely the assumption would be, if there was no answer to his knocking, that there would be no-one at home ?"

" Who told you that he broke down the door ?" asked Lestrade in some surprise.

" Why, our very own Sunday-school Albert Stevens," Holmes answered him. " He told us that fact had been re-ported in the newspapers, but as I remember, it was not in the report that we read."

" It was not," I confirmed.

" And nor would it have been," Lestrade answered Holmes, " unless one of my constables has been speaking to the news-papers out of turn. George Timmins claims that he went to the house, and knocked on the door. To his surprise, it swung open, having been previously forced open by person or per-sons unknown. He thereupon entered the house, and liter-ally stumbled over the body of the younger girl, which was lying just inside the front door. On proceeding further, he encountered the other corpses, whereupon he summoned a constable. This is all according to his version of events, you understand."

" And in your opinion ?"

Lestrade laughed mirthlessly. " I think it is obvious, Mr. Holmes. Timmins broke down the door himself, though we were unable to get him to admit to having done such a thing. He thereupon slew the four victims, for reasons as yet unknown to us."

" At what time does he say he discovered the bodies ?" Holmes asked.

" A little after quarter-past three," replied the police agent.

" Then, my dear Lestrade, you may well find this to be of some interest," Holmes told him, producing from his pocket the copy of the Times which he had been studying earlier, and which contained the advertisement in the agony column.

Lestrade studied it, frowning. " This is gibberish,

Mr. Holmes. I assume that you believe it contains some sense ?"

" Indeed it does. It is a relatively trivial cypher, and the decoded version is here." He handed a slip of paper from his pocketbook to Lestrade, who scanned it.

" Well, assuming that your interpretation of this message is correct, and that we have that would seem to indicate that Timmins was expecting to meet someone, and if the meeting did not take place at the place specified, he would have a reason to enter the house. I think that we now definitely have the murderer, thanks to you, Mr. Holmes."

" Why, in your opinion, do you think he killed the family ?" I asked Lestrade.

" A falling-out between thieves," said Lestrade. " Let us assume that the arranged meeting was for the purpose of selling stolen goods. Timmins arrives with the stolen goods at the appointed time and place, fails to meet MS, whom we may well assume, as do you, may be identified with Mary Stevens. What does he do ? He goes to the house, opens the door, whether or not it is locked, since he is an accomplished housebreaker, and meets Mrs. Stevens. An altercation ensues, and becomes violent, resulting in the death of Mary Stevens. Timmins turns and observes that the three children have been witnesses to the crime. What is his answer ? He must kill them all, swiftly and surely. He then leaves the house, putting the door on the sneck, and proceeds to ' discover' the bodies, breaking down the door to do so."

" An excellent theory, Lestrade. I must applaud you," said Holmes. " However, I fear we should examine the circumstances a little more, especially this matter of Albert Stevens' alibi."

" I admit that it is strange that a man who claims to be worried about possible arrest and conviction for murder should forget his alibi."

" Would you have any objection if I were to investigate that side of the problem ?" Holmes asked politely.

" By no means, Mr. Holmes."

" And have you discovered the murder weapon ?"

Lestrade shook his head. " Almost certainly at the bottom of the Thames by now."

With that, Holmes and I set off for the premises of Richardson & Co., which Stevens had informed us were his employers. We were introduced to Mr. Charles Hargreaves, who was given out as being in charge of the clerks employed by the firm.

The name of Albert Stevens produced a frown of anger. " Why yes, indeed I remember him well. We have very little trouble with most of our employees. Though I say it myself, I am a good judge of character, but in the case of this young man, it would seem that I made one of the biggest mistakes of my life."

" How so ?" asked Holmes.

" The wretched youth turned out to be a thief. Some fifty guineas or so in cash went missing, and all the evidence pointed to him as the culprit. Indeed, there is no way that the theft could have been perpetrated by anyone other than him."

" But you did not prosecute ?" I asked.

Hargreaves shook his head. " He had left the firm some months before the theft was discovered. It had been carried out in a most ingenious manner, such that it would not be noticed until the six-month reconciliation of accounts. There is no doubt that it was Stevens who was responsible."

" But you did not call in the police ?" Holmes enquired.

" We wished to avoid adverse publicity. Our clients repose a certain amount of trust in us as purveyors of insurance. To admit that we had suffered a loss which went unremarked for a matter of months would destroy that trust, and would almost certainly lose us business. We therefore decided to keep the matter quiet, and to let sleeping dogs lie. The amount, though not trifling, was not of an amount that would materially affect our business."

" You say that he left some months before the theft was discovered ? When exactly did you notice that the money was missing ?"

" It was some nine months ago that we noticed the discrepancy, and if my memory serves me rightly, Stevens left us some two months prior to that with good references, written by myself, I am ashamed to say"

" So he has not been working here for close on a year ?"

" That is correct. I can examine the records and discover the exact date on which he left us, if you can wait a few minutes," suggested the elderly clerk.

" That will not be necessary, thank you, Mr. Hargreaves," Holmes told him pleasantly. " You have been most helpful. My sincere thanks."

" Well, Watson, what should we make of all that ?" smiled Holmes, as we strolled along the London streets.

" It seems extraordinary to me that he should engage in such a falsehood ; one which is so easily detected as such."

" It may be that he considered his appearance, which he believed to present a facade of respectability, would not cause us to question him. But it now seems to me that we have a most unsavoury threesome in this case : namely, Mr. Stevens, his late wife, and this Timmins, all of whom are known to have engaged in criminal activities of one kind or another. There is one more point that may be worthy of mention."

" That being ?"

" We were just informed that Stevens carried out his depredations a year ago, and if you remember, Stevens himself informed us that he married his late wife at about the same time. Should we suspect a coincidence, or a link between these two events ?"

" Given your remark the other day regarding coincidences, I would say the latter."

Holmes chuckled. " I also. This case has the makings of a pretty little puzzle, does it not ?"

My friend was in high good humour as we strolled the streets of London on our way back to Baker-street, remarking on the probable occupations of those whom we encountered. " A cobbler, if I am not mistaken," he observed of one such. " Note the worn patch on the knee of the trouser where he holds his last, and that unusual hunch of the shoulders which is peculiar to that trade."

Naturally, I had no way of confirming Holmes' deductions, but it seemed to me to be more likely than otherwise that he was correct in his deductions. Indeed, I made a few ventures myself in that area, and was gratified to note my companion's nods of approval.

" You are surely coming on apace, Watson," he remarked to me when we were safely ensconced in our chairs in our Baker-street rooms. " I will be able to retire soon, and hand my work over to you."

" Hardly," I laughed. " I do not see your mental engine racing furiously with no work to give it. I believe that you will remain in full employment for the foreseeable future."

" You are correct, for the moment at least. However, it seems to me that a quiet retirement in a rural area, such as the Sussex Downs, would be an appropriate way to meet the end of my time on this earth, with some new skill or pastime to occupy my mind. I confess to be fascinated by the habits of bees and the little societies that they inhabit."

" I can hardly picture you in that bucolic setting," I retorted. " You are a creature of the city, and I believe you would suffocate were you removed from the smoke and fogs of the metropolis, which are as necessary to your existence as is oxygen to other mortals."

Holmes smiled. " You know me too well, Watson. But, to work, and less of these fancies. Let us look at that message in the agony column. Do you remember how it was signed ? ' Love and godspeed' were the words used. To my mind, that suggests a substantially closer relationship between the two parties than that of housebreaker and ' fence'. Shall we make our way to Bermondsey tomorrow morning ?"

" What do you expect to discover there ?"

" I am not sure, but I am convinced that whatever is there will help to shed more light on the mystery."

Accordingly, the next morning saw us at the mean little house in Webster Street. As had been arranged the previous evening, Lestrade was waiting for us.

" We have Timmins," were his first words to us on meeting. " We pulled him in last night."

" You are convinced of his guilt ?"

" Of the murder here, no," Lestrade confessed to us. " However, we are certain of his having even involved in a housebreaking in Pimlico last week. Some of the items which had been stolen from the house in Warwick Square were in his possession. There is no doubt that these monogrammed pieces of plate are the same as those reported as having been taken."

" And he has confessed to the theft ?"

" By no means," answered Lestrade, shaking his head. " You would imagine, would you not, that confronted with such clear evidence of his guilt, that he would admit his crime. But no, he sings the old familiar song, and claims that he has no idea how the spoons and coffee-pot came to be under his bed."

" Has he said any more about his relationship with the dead woman, Mrs. Stevens ?"

" Only what we had already confirmed some time ago at the

time of his arrest and hers. The two cases were linked, do you know, with the loot from his robbery going to her."

Holmes repeated the words with which the message in the agony column had been signed, and ended by remarking that this would argue a closer relationship between Timmins and Mary Stevens than had previously been assumed.

" Given, of course, that the initials in that message correspond to the principals in this case," Lestrade pointed out.

" Given that fact, naturally," agreed Holmes. " Let us examine the door which Timmins alleges he did not force open, and which you believe he broke down." So saying, he moved to the front door of the house, which appeared to have suffered some recent damage to the door itself, and to the frame. " Is he a big man ?"

" I would say so. Nearly as tall as you, Mr. Holmes, and considerably broader and heavier, and in excellent physical condition. I believe he would have little difficulty in using his muscles to force open a door such as this."

" But of course, our Mr. Stevens is of much slighter build," mused Holmes, half to himself.

" Your meaning ?"

" See here." Holmes pointed to a series of marks on the door frame. " Had the door been burst open by brute force, such as would be used by a large strong man such as Timmins, I would expect to see signs of strain on the screws fixing the lock to the door, here, and here. Instead of which, it is clear that a crowbar has been used to force the door open. You may observe the marks of the crowbar here, and the resulting strain on the bolts here." He indicated two further points on the frame.

Lestrade bent to examine the points mentioned by Holmes, and straightened with a grunt. " I dare say you are correct, Mr. Holmes," he said. " But if I read your words aright, you are implying that Stevens forced open his own door with a crowbar, even though he like as not had a key in his pocket, and his wife and children were inside should he by chance have forgotten a key. Why in the world would a man break down his own front door ?"

" I have my ideas," smiled Holmes. " Shall we see inside the house ?"

The bodies of Mrs. Stevens and the children had, of course, been removed, but chalk marks on the bare boards indicated where the results of the tragedy had taken place.

" What of the causes of death ?" I asked Lestrade.

" Injuries to the head. In the case of Mary Stevens, the injuries were repeated and particularly brutal. All appeared to have been inflicted by some blunt instrument."

" Such as a crowbar ?" suggested Holmes.

Lestrade looked at Holmes with an expression of incredulity. " I hardly know what you are suggesting there, Mr. Holmes."

" I hardly know myself," said my friend. " That is to say, I cannot pronounce with any certainty on the facts of the matter, but I have more than one theory rattling around in my head at present."

" You are too much for me," smiled Lestrade. " I take it that you will wish to see Timmins ? We have him in the cells at Bow-street, and he won't be going away from there in a hurry, you may be certain of that."

" All in good time. For now, Watson and I will be going to Lafone Street, Southwark. There is a small matter about which I wish to be certain."

" Very well. I will see you later, Mr. Holmes, and Dr. Watson. You have once again set me on a track other than the one I had firmly believed to be correct."

" And it will not be the last time that I set Lestrade straight on a case, or I am a Dutchman," muttered Holmes, sotto voce, as we turned the corner towards Southwark.

As I had surmised, our port of call was Lightfoot & Sons, which had been given by Albert Stevens as his alibi. Once more we were faced with a specimen of the genus that I might term " elderly senior clerk", this time by the name of Daniel Pincher.

" Yes, I remember young Stevens coming in to collect the insurance premium for Richardson's the other day. He was in here at about three o'clock, or a little before. Actually, now I come to recall the matter, the appointment was for three o'clock, but he arrived at half-past two. He took the money from me, which I had ready, prepared in an envelope—"

" About how much money was involved ?" asked Holmes.

" Twenty-three guineas. It is an expensive sum to be paying every six months, to be sure, but our premium covers all risks, including the loss of cargo in transit from America to here. Mr. Stevens has been collecting it from us in person for the past two years, since Richardson's changed their *modus operandi*. Previously we sent a cheque to them, but they cited banking charges as the reason for the change to cash, to be delivered to them by one of their trusted employees."

I could not prevent myself from smiling inwardly at this description of Stevens, who had shown himself to be so untrustworthy to his erstwhile employers.

" A cool customer, that," remarked Holmes, as we took the hansom cab to Bow-street. " Collecting insurance premiums for a company that ceased to employ him nearly a year ago. A novelty in the annals of crime, in my experience at least, though I remember Groschen mentioning a similar case in Graz some years back."

On arrival at Bow-street, we were conducted to the cell where George Timmins was being held. As Lestrade had previously informed us, he was little short of being a giant of a man, with Holmes' height, and considerably more than his bulk. To me, it appeared ludicrous that such a man would use a crowbar to open a locked door, when a mere tap from his fist would seemingly be sufficient.

" What are you here for ? " were his first words to us, uttered in a truculent tone. " And who the deuce are you, anyway ? "

" My name is Sherlock Holmes, and this is my friend and colleague, Dr. Watson."

" I've read of you in the papers, Mr. Sherlock Holmes. You're the cove what puts poor innocents like me in the clink, aren't you ? "

" Mr. Timmins," Holmes replied calmly. " I assure you that I am only interested in assuring myself, and the police, of the truth. And in your case, I believe the truth is something other than that which the police currently believe. With your assistance, I feel I can persuade them to come round to my way of thinking."

Timing appeared to consider this for a moment, then burst out laughing. " You're a right card, you are, Mr. Holmes. I suppose you want to ask me a few questions, don't you ? "

" Indeed I do. I knew you'd turn out to be an intelligent man, Mr. Timmins." Timmins fairly beamed at this praise. " First, let me hear from your own lips that you are innocent."

" Of what, Mr. Holmes ? Of the job in Warwick Square, which is why I'm here, or of the killing of poor Mary and her little ones, which is what they pulled me in for to start with, and then had to let me go ? "

" Why, both, if you would be so kind."

" Strewth. No-one like you's ever talked to me like that before. It's a real pleasure to be chatting with you, sir," said Timmins, and I knew that Holmes' charm, which he could deploy like a weapon when he chose, had had its effect on the rogue. " Why, sir, I'm innocent of both of them. I've done things in my time, sir, but these two aren't on that list. I'll take my oath on that."

" I believe you," said Holmes, simply, and again I could see that the courtesy with which he treated Timmins was working its magic. " Tell me, you knew Mary Stevens well ?"

" Don't call her by that name. Mary Holt she was when I first knew her, and Mary Holt she will always be to me. Her three little ones, I can tell you now, sir, they were mine. I loved that woman, sir, I did, and now she's gone, she and Bessie and Janie and little Georgie. We first met when she fenced the swag from one of the jobs I did some twenty years back." He paused and addressed Holmes with an air of great seriousness. " Tell me, sir, do you believe in love at first sight ?"

The idea of this bearded ruffian asking such a question of Sherlock Holmes nearly caused me to erupt in a spasm of incongruous merriment, but Holmes treated the question with all seriousness.

" I have not experienced the emotion at first hand, Mr. Timmins, but I can assure you that I have observed it in others, more than once. I take it that you and Mary Holt felt this way about each other ?"

" We did indeed, Mr. Holmes. She was everything to me, and I believed I was everything to her, until that Bert Stevens came along with his cash. Turned up on her doorstep somehow, and with this big envelope full of Bank of England five-pound notes which he wouldn't tell anybody where they'd come from. I never thought my Mary could be bought, but God help me, he bought her, that little shrimp of a lily-livered excuse for a man. They were married inside the month." Here, Timmins gulped with emotion and, rogue that he was, I could not help feeling more than a little pity for him. " But Mary still was still in the fencing trade, and she still took my swag from me when I'd cracked a case. And she was still sweet on me, I could tell that. I don't need to tell you gents what I felt for her."

" And what did Stevens have to say about this ?" Holmes asked.

" He never knew anything. Too wrapped up in his own games, he was, to care about Mary and me. At least, that's what her and me thought. All he wanted was a roof over his head, away from the rozzers. Mary used to send me messages in the *Times*, would you believe that ? A toff's paper, and she sent me messages."

" I know," said Holmes, smiling. " The code was not a difficult one."

Timmins smiled. " I'd heard you was clever, sir. Well, sir, that Bert Stevens was pretty clever, too, and it was him who put out a message in what we thought was our private code, from Mary, as I thought, asking me to meet her at the end of the road. Is that one that you saw ?" Holmes nodded. " The idea was to get me there at the time that he killed Mary and the little ones."

" And his motive for killing her ? Why would he do that ?"

" He was jealous, sir. Jealous of what Mary and I felt for each other. Different to what we'd thought. He reckoned he'd bought Mary, see, and she was still sweet on me, and that hurt his pride. So she had to go, and as a final piece of his devil's work, I had to be hanged for the crime he had committed. I couldn't say nothing to the rozzers about any of this. They wouldn't understand. But you, sir, you seem to know what I'm talking about."

" And the children ? Why did they have to die ?"

" My Bessie, my Janie and my little George ? God knows, Mr. Holmes. I hope you can find out. Maybe they witnessed him killing my Mary and had to go in their turn ? Maybe they were a reminder of what we had shared together ? If you find out, sir, let me know, please. I'm not a religious man, sir, but as soon as they let me out after bringing me in for the murders, I went into a church, which is something I haven't done since I was a nipper, and I lit a candle to Mary. For my Mary, and our three children." There were tears in the big man's eyes as he recounted these words.

" Mr Timmins," Holmes said, following a long silence. " You are either the greatest actor on God's good earth, or you are telling me the absolute truth. I believe the latter. We have already established that Stevens is a liar and a fraud, and it takes little more to see him as a murderer. I have little difficulty in believing the truth of what you have told me, and I feel I will have little difficulty in persuading the police of the truth of your case. One more question. What of the items from Warwick Square that were discovered in your lodgings ?"

" I'm innocent of that, sir. I've cracked a few cribs, as I'm sure you know, but not that one. I swear that to you, Mr. Holmes."

" I believe you," Holmes said, once again, and the simplicity and obvious sincerity of his answer caused the other to extend his hand.

" You're a gentleman, Mr. Sherlock Holmes, and don't let anyone ever tell you any different. I give you my hand, sir, in friendship, and I swear to you, because of what you are and what you have said to me just now, I'll keep to the right side of the law from now on, so strike me dead if I don't."

Holmes grasped the proffered hand, and grasped it firmly. " Thank you, Mr. Timmins," he said, and I swear that on this occasion, Sherlock Holmes, the great calculating detective, was far from unmoved. As for me, I do not trust myself to record my feelings on this occasion.

On leaving the cell, Holmes sought out Lestrade, and confronted him with what we had just learned.

" I am to understand," said the police agent, " that Stevens returned to his home, having previously established an unreliable alibi, and beat his wife to death with a crowbar, on account of her previous liaison with Timmins ?"

" Precisely so. The children witnessed this abominable act, and thereupon met their deaths. Even a worm may become dangerous when turned, and this worm Stevens had indeed turned. Whereupon, he left the house, locking the door on the sneck behind him, and forced it open, using the same vile instrument with which he had just taken the lives of four human beings. You remarked the traces of blood and hair on the doorframe where the crowbar had been employed ? No ?"

" And Timmins ?"

" Was summoned by a message placed in the agony column of the Times by Stevens, using the supposedly secret code employed by Timmins and his inamorata. The intention was to lead him to Webster Street, and to enter the house, where he would thereupon become the prime suspect with regard to the murders."

" And the plate from Warwick Square ?"

" My belief, though this may be confirmed by Stevens, is that it was fenced by another housebreaker through Mary Stevens, as I suppose we must call her. Stevens took it, and, having ascertained Timmins' address, contrived to place it there, in a location where it was not to be discovered at a casual glance, but where it was sure to be discovered in a police search."

Lestrade sighed. " It all makes sense," he admitted. " And I suppose we must let Timmins go free."

" Do so," Holmes told him, " and you will be freeing a man whose earnest wish, I strongly believe, is to live an honest life from now on."

" I had never trusted Stevens from the time he walked into our room," said Holmes to me, after he had read the account of the trial and conviction of Albert Stevens for the murder of his wife and her three children, in which Inspector Lestrade of Scotland Yard was praised for his powers of observation and induction which had led to the identifying of the true perpetrator of this abominable crime.

" Why is that ?" I asked.

" Elementary," replied my friend. " He was dressed all in mourning black, was he not ? But in his pocket was the programme of a music-hall performance from the previous evening. What sort of man discovers his slaughtered wife and step-children, and then proceeds to spend the evening at a music-hall ? At that moment, I knew that all was not that it might be."

THE ADVENTURE OF THE GREEN DRAGON

"He is a big, powerful chap, clean-shaven, and very swarthy something like Aldridge, who helped us in the bogus laundry affair."

The Adventure of the Cardboard Box

AVE you ever heard," Sherlock Holmes once asked me, " of the Salisbury Rub ?"

" Indeed I have not."

" It refers to a somewhat unsavoury and painful tactic in boxing, that is to say, the genus of the sport that is practiced in the back rooms of public houses, and in deserted barns where the serious followers of the Fancy gather."

" And in which you yourself have taken part ?"

" I confess that in my younger days, the fights in which I distinguished myself were not always conducted according to the Queensbury Rules. But those days are behind me."

" And did you ever administer this 'Salisbury Rub' to an opponent."

" Indeed not. It would have been unworthy of me to do so. I was the intended victim of the move on a couple of occasions, however, and only fast footwork saved me from incurring a seriously disfiguring permanent injury as a result."

" Let us be thankful for that," I answered. " But tell me, why do you ask ?"

" I know that my visitor later this afternoon has suffered from his opponent inflicting the Rub on him at some time in the past and it has left its mark on him. I would ask you to show no surprise or make any reference to it. Mr. Jim Aldridge is still a force to be reckoned with, physically at least. Years in the ring have, I fear, produced no improvement to his mental faculties, which were never his forte in the first place. He was always known for his short temper, and the years have not brought an amelioration in that regard, either."

" Then I should go ?"

" By no means, my dear man. If you stay in your capacity as a medical man and observe what manner of ills may befall one who takes up the life of a sportsman, you may increase your sphere of knowledge."

" I cannot say that I am anticipating the visit of this Mr. Aldridge with any pleasure, after what you have just told me."

" Oh, come. He is a perfectly amiable dolt for the most part, unless crossed."

" And why is he coming here ?"

" Ah, now that is more to my taste than the man himself, believe me. He sent a message through Wiggins, claiming to have something that will be of interest to me. I have no idea what it is to which he is referring, and with the criminals of the metropolis seemingly taking their leisure, I am currently at a loose end, and would welcome any diversion such as this. Ha ! I believe I hear his tread now."

Without Holmes' warning, I would have certainly let out a cry of surprise at the appearance of the man who entered our Baker-street rooms. He was a large man, powerfully built, and swarthy in his general appearance, and might almost have been considered handsome had his left eye not been disfigured by an evil-looking scar which crossed his face from forehead to cheekbone, taking in his eyelid. I shuddered inwardly at the thought of the blow that must have caused this disfigurement, but, remembering Holmes' words, betrayed as little of my feelings as possible.

" Mr. 'Olmes," he fluted in a small piping voice that was at odds with his overall appearance. " 'Appy to make your acquaintance once more. It must be ten years since we last met."

" Nine years, ten months and thirteen days, to be precise," Holmes smiled. " Won't you sit down, Jim ?"

" 'Oo's 'e ?" asked Aldridge, jabbing a gnarled thumb in my direction.

" This is Doctor Watson, my friend and colleague, who assists me in my work."

" And you're some sort of private bobby now, I hear from that lad I run into ?"

Holmes nodded. " That will serve as a description."

" Then you'll like as not be interested in this." He reached in the pocket of his shabby coat, and produced what I took to be a handkerchief, seemingly cleaner than what I would have expected, which he then proceeded to unfold. " 'Ere you are, Mr. 'Olmes," he told my friend, holding out a scarred hand, in the palm of which reposed a small object. " Feast your eyes on that."

Holmes took the object and held it up to his eye before reaching for a lens and examining it more closely. He let out a long low whistle. " Do you know what you have there, Jim ?"

Our visitor shook his head.

" It is a scarf pin, and if I am not mistaken, it belongs to the Earl of Scarborough. I was informed of its loss last week. Hmm." He examined the handkerchief. " Most interesting. The carving of the jade head is exquisite. See for yourself, Watson. Such workmanship is the product of a few locations in China, where this undoubtedly originated. This really is most interesting, Jim," he repeated. " Thank you for bringing it to me."

" The pin ?"

" No, no. The handkerchief. The pin I knew already, but the handkerchief is new to me, of course."

" You knew about the pin already ? It's worth something, then ?"

" It's worth a lot of money, Jim. How did you come by it ?"

" I found it in the street."

Sherlock Holmes smiled indulgently. " Come now, do you expect me to believe that ?"

" It's the truth, Mr. 'Olmes, I swear it. God's truth. I was walking along the Mile End-road, when a cart went by with a great clatter as it turned the corner going up towards the West End. It turned so fast that the horse had to pull up, and I went over to lend a hand. Well, they went off all right again, but when I looked down, there was this on the ground, next to this handkerchief, of all things. At first I thought it was just a bit of stone, but then when I looked at it a bit more. I thought what you just said, that it was something valuable."

" Very interesting," said Holmes. " Can you describe the cart ?"

Aldridge scratched his head in thought. " Can't say that I can. Horse was a roan, driver could have been anyone."

" You wouldn't know him again ?"

" No. I hardly saw his face. Now I come to think of it, he had a scarf around his face, and you couldn't hardly make out anything, except his eyes between the scarf and his cap. Dark eyes, they were. Mind you, he was busy with the cart, I was busy with the horse." He paused for a moment. " You say this belongs to some toff ?"

" I believe so," answered Holmes.

" Then I can't keep it ?" Aldridge's face fell.

" It would be as well to give it to the police. I will make sure you get a reward." Aldridge seemed to brighten at this news. " Was there anything else with the pin when you discovered it ?"

" The handkerchief I was carrying that pin in, what you've got now. And a sock."

" Do you still have the sock ? "

" Brought it with me. "

" Hand it over, would you ? " Holmes asked him.

" One sock ? You're barmy, Mr. 'Olmes, you are. " He smilingly handed over the object to Holmes, who placed it on one side after examining it briefly.

" If the villain who stole this pin is arrested, I will make sure you receive your reward. Come now, " he added, as Aldridge visibly turned the matter over in his mind. " This is a valuable piece. You can't fence it, and if you try, you won't get half of what the reward money will be. "

" How much ? "

" I would expect you to receive not less than ten pounds. "

" You're right, Mr. 'Olmes. I confess I did take it to a fence, and he offered me four pound ten for it. Ten sounds better. "

" One more thing, Jim. I want you to tell this story to the police. Don't worry, I am not going to mention the little affair of Beckstall Street. "

" How the Devil do you know of that ? " Aldridge asked, with a visible start.

" It is my business to know of these things, " Holmes answered evenly. " But I see no reason to share my knowledge with others always. "

" You always was a smart 'un, Mr. 'Olmes. So you want me to go to the police and tell them what I just told you ? "

" I will accompany you, Jim. The police inspector I have in mind to hear your story will listen to you if I am with you, and I will be able to persuade him to obtain the reward money for you. Doctor Watson will accompany us, will you not ? " he added, turning to me.

" Of course, " I replied.

At Scotland Yard, Inspector Stanley Hopkins examined the pin, and pronounced it as his opinion that the item indeed corresponded to the description of the scarf pin that had been reported by the Earl of Scarborough as being stolen. He listened to the story told by Aldridge with an air of immense scepticism, but allowed himself to be persuaded of its veracity by Holmes.

On hearing my friend's insistence that Aldridge receive a reward, he readily assented to exert himself to obtain this from the Earl.

" If you could keep your eyes open for that cart," he told Aldridge, " and let me know if you see it again, I will be most grateful."

" I can't promise anything, but I'll do what I can," Aldridge told him. " How will I get the money for that pin, though ?"

" Come round to Baker-street next Thursday," said Holmes. " I'll make sure you get your money."

" Well, thank you, gents," Aldridge said to us, since the conversation now appeared to be at an end. " I'll be off now. I haven't told Mr. 'Olmes where he can find me, but I'd lay money he knows anyway."

Holmes said nothing, but smiled as Aldridge took his leave of us.

" What is going on ?" I demanded of Holmes and Hopkins. " Why all this fuss about one pin ?"

" In the first place, my dear Watson, it is an extremely valuable pin. The jade carving in the head has been valued at some thousands of pounds, has it not, Inspector ? It is a unique example of the craftsman's skill and diligence."

" Indeed it has been valued very highly. According to the Earl, it is indeed unique, and it would be impossible to set a price on it." Hopkins confirmed. " However, it is but one of many small trinkets that have been reported missing over the past few months."

" All from the same household ?" I asked.

" Not at all," Holmes answered me. " Hopkins here came

to me a month ago with a complete list of the objects that have gone missing. I have it here, and you will notice that they have been lost from about twenty different households." He passed a piece of paper to me.

" And they are all small objects, such as this scarf-pin, or a snuff-box or a brooch," I remarked, after looking through the list.

" You will also notice," Hopkins pointed out, " that none of these items is valued at less than one thousand pounds."

" But surely," I objected, " such items are lost regularly, are they not ?"

" They may well be," Hopkins told me, " but if that is the case, they are not reported to us, as these have been. This list represents a positive flood, if that is the correct word, of missing items, which is totally unprecedented in all my years on the Force."

" And I assume that there has been no sign of any entry to the houses from which they have been found to be missing ?"

" Precisely so. If there had been a wave of housebreaking, then that would have been unwelcome, but not unusual news," Holmes said to me.

" And the offenders would be behind bars by now," Hopkins added.

" Maybe," smiled Holmes. " I am of the opinion that the truth of that statement would depend on whether you had sought my assistance or not. In any event, the question is a theoretical one, since it appears that housebreaking is not part of the thieves' modus operandi."

" Then," I reasoned, " we must suspect the servants."

" Naturally," said Hopkins. " That is the line of enquiry that we have been pursuing, with the help of Mr. Holmes here."

I had been unaware that my friend had been engaged in any such activity, and I regarded him quizzically. The answer I received to my unspoken enquiry was the familiar half-raised eyebrow, and the corners of his mouth twitched slightly. I had noticed his disappearance from our Baker-street rooms at irregular intervals, usually clad in garments that suggested a lower social status, but he had heretofore refused to answer my queries regarding his departures or arrivals at odd times of the day or night.

" Can you be certain that the servants are innocent ?" I asked Holmes.

" I cannot be completely certain," he admitted, " but I cannot fathom how the servants from all these houses could have had access to these items, and then removed them from the house. It is possible, I agree, but unlikely that the same method has been used in each case."

" You have remarked to me in the past that whenever the impossible has been eliminated, whatever remains, however improbable—"

" Indeed, Watson," he said to me, somewhat testily. " However, the fact remains that this scarf pin is the first item on this list to be located."

" Which means, in my opinion at any rate, that these things are being taken out of the country and being sold," interjected Hopkins.

" I had reached that conclusion myself," said Holmes, with a touch of asperity. " But how and where are they being passed over ?"

" That's the mystery," Hopkins agreed. " We set a little trap in one of the houses where one of these things had gone missing in the past. The bait vanished, but we knew there was only the one person, the lady's maid, who could have taken it. My men followed her around for two weeks on her days off, but there was no-one to whom she could have passed it."

" Other than her young man," Holmes corrected him,

" whom she accompanied to the Criterion on the Saturday afternoon."

" My man did not see you there," said Hopkins, obviously surprised at Holmes' words.

" I took good care that he should not. I take it that you have investigated that young man, by the way ?"

" Yes, and he remains our prime suspect. He has been observed on several occasions in areas of London where we would not expect a stockbroker's clerk to visit."

" Such as the Mile End-road ?" Holmes asked.

" Indeed so."

" So your supposition is that Mr. Leighton Harrison received the stolen – brooch, was it not ? – from his young lady, and took it to the East End, from where it was conveniently disposed of through the denizens of the docks ?"

" Absolutely, Mr. Holmes. In fact, we intend to pull him in and ask him to whom he gave the brooch."

Holmes shook his head. " You will be wasting your time, Inspector. Firstly, I can almost promise you that even if he were guilty of involvement in this case, you would be unable to obtain any information from him that would aid you in your enquiries. If the gang involved have been clever enough to organise some kind of robbery involving twenty different households, they will certainly be sufficiently capable of hiding their identities from their confederates."

" You seem to be sure of his innocence," I said.

" I can confidently state that he will deny any charge you may bring before him with regard to that brooch, and he will deny it for the best of reasons."

" That being ?" asked Hopkins.

" That he is innocent of the crime. I will wager that he knows nothing of it. I have already ascertained that fact."

" Then you have alerted him that we are on his trail !"

exclaimed Hopkins angrily. " This is hardly helpful to our enquiries, Mr. Holmes."

" Softly, Inspector." Holmes held up a warning hand. " I did not approach Harrison in my own person, but as a possible buyer of any items that he might have acquired through less than legal means. He rebuffed me in such a manner that I was fully persuaded that he was innocent of any wrongdoing. Indeed, it was with the greatest of difficulty that I prevented him from calling one of your constables and giving me in charge."

" Well, I suppose we will have to take your word on that, Mr. Holmes."

" Maybe I can add one more link to your chain of reasoning, Hopkins. To employ a separate courier, such as you are suspecting, for every house from which objects have been purloined, would seem to increase the possibility of discovery considerably. I do not think that this gang would engage in this undertaking with such a risk hanging over their heads. And Harrison would appear to be devoted solely to the good Lily, and displays no interest in other women."

" Very well, then," grumbled Hopkins. " I will take your word for it. I cannot say that I am altogether happy with what you have been doing, however."

" Rather, Inspector," Holmes called over his shoulder as we turned to leave Scotland Yard, " you should be thankful that I have saved you from making an embarrassing blunder that might have reflected badly on your future career."

" Believe me, Watson," Holmes said to me as we walked back to Baker-street. " I had no wish to involve you in this affair when Hopkins first requested my assistance. With all due respect to your abilities, you would have been unable to produce the results that I have achieved so far. However," and here he rubbed his hands together, " Jim Aldridge has produced something of great value, and even if it means I shall have to pay it myself, he shall be rewarded for it."

" You refer to the scarf pin ?"

" No, no, not at all. I refer to the handkerchief and the sock. The scarf pin was well-known to us before. The handkerchief and sock are important clues. When we return to Baker-street, you may examine them and deduce what you will from them."

Some thirty minutes later, I laid the articles aside, having examined them with the aid of one of Holmes' lenses.

" The handkerchief is obviously that of a woman," I said. " The sock is a man's. Both appear to be of good quality, and therefore may be considered to be expensive. Other than that, I am unable to draw any conclusions."

Holmes laughed and shook his head. " My dear fellow, you have failed to draw the most elementary conclusions from these objects."

" Those being ?" I asked, not a little nettled.

" Firstly, you will observe the state of these items. They are clean, are they not ?"

" Indeed so."

" Not only are they clean, but in the case of the handkerchief, starched and ironed. Now, I must ask you, on what occasion would a clean man's sock, a singleton at that, and a lady's handkerchief of this quality, also clean, and starched into the bargain, find themselves in close proximity in the Mile End-road ?"

" I cannot conceive of any such."

" Let us assume that they are being returned from a laundry in the East End."

" That would certainly appear to meet the facts as we know them," I admitted.

" Let us expand on my little supposition. Let us assume

that the cart that Aldridge encountered was a laundry cart, transporting items to and from a laundry somewhere in the East End. In addition to its cargo or items of clothing, I think we may assume that it was also carrying the pin, as it had carried the other items out of the houses from which they had been purloined, and thence to the collector of these things, who would then deliver the clean garments to their rightful owners, while retaining the pin and other things. Who would ever look for missing jewellery in a laundry basket being carried out of the house ? It is true that the basket might well be searched when the object was first missed, but it would be the work of a moment to slip the jade pin, for example, into the basket as it was carried out of the house."

" You see everything, Holmes."

" On the contrary, you see everything that I do. You merely fail to draw the obvious conclusions."

" I fail to see that this deduction of yours leads us towards the stolen items, though."

" Surely you observed the laundry mark on the handkerchief. It will be possible, though tedious, to match this mark with those employed by a laundry in the area of the cart encountered by Aldridge, and hence run the perpetrators to earth. Before proceeding with this, however, it might be advisable to collect a few more such marks from other households where items have gone missing, simply to establish the fact that all make use of the services provided by the same laundry."

" That is surely something with which I can be of assistance ?" I asked. " My practice is currently undemanding, and I would welcome a break from the imagined medical problems of elderly spinsters."

" Very well, then. Your help will be most welcome. I will make a list of houses for you to visit. You should ask the housekeeper if you may examine the handkerchiefs that have recently been returned from the laundry, and make an exact copy of any marks you may see on them."

At the end of the next day, I returned to Baker-street, having visited some half a dozen of the houses from which items had been reported as missing. Holmes, who had been engaged in some chemical research in connection with another case, took one look at my face, and sank back in his chair.

" It is evident that you discovered nothing," he remarked.

" It is not that I discovered nothing. I discovered too much."

" Why, what can you mean ?"

" The laundry marks in the different houses all differ one from another. And yet, when I asked the housekeepers in each house, they all gave me the same name of the enterprise employed by the household, that is to say, the Eastside Laundry, located in an area between Whitechapel and Stepney."

" Well done, Watson !" Holmes exclaimed. " You have solved the whole mystery in a day. All the credit shall be yours."

" Mine ? How have I solved the problem ?" I demanded in some perplexity.

" Never mind that. You have the address of this Eastside Laundry ?"

" I do," I told him.

" Then let us go there. Come."

We took a hansom to Whitechapel and commenced our walk along the Mile End-road. " The second street on the left, I believe," said Holmes after a few minutes. I had occasion in the past to remark Holmes' almost uncanny knowledge of the geography of the metropolis, but it never failed to amaze and impress me.

Sure enough, after taking the turning that Holmes had indicated, we soon came to a door on which was emblazoned

" Eastside Laundry". There were few windows, and such that existed were heavily barred.

" Odd," said Holmes, sniffing the air. " One would expect a building marked as a laundry to show some signs of use as such. This would appear to be an ordinary dwelling, and certainly not an establishment capable of handling the requirements of several large households. The place has an almost fortified air to it, would you not agree ?"

He rapped on the door with his stick, and after a minute or two, it was opened by one who appeared to be a Chinaman.

" He no here !" the Oriental told us, before Holmes or I had even opened our mouths. " He come back next week, next month, next year, maybe. He never say me when he come and go. Come back then and go now !"

And with that, the door was slammed in our faces. We could hear the sound of keys turning in locks, and bars being thrown up.

" Well," laughed Holmes. " I have to say I never expected a welcome such as that."

" Our visit seems to have been a waste of time, then," I said. " Other than the fact that there is at least one Chinaman involved in the case."

" By no means a waste of time," replied my friend. " We know that there is something very strange indeed about the Eastside Laundry, do we not ? It seems to be a legitimate business, taking in dirty laundry from households, and delivering it cleaned and pressed. The housekeepers to whom you spoke expressed their satisfaction with the services they received, did they not ?"

" But no laundry business is carried out there," I objected.

" Naturally. The address we have just visited serves merely as a repository for the objects pilfered from the houses. The actual laundry is carried out by other firms."

" And what of the Chinaman ?"

Holmes shrugged. " He would seem to be a pawn of the prime movers of this little game, would he not ? The 'he' to whom he referred is presumably the leader of this operation, and the man through whom all the stolen goods pass." We resumed our return journey to Baker-street, Holmes seemingly deep in thought.

" I will ask Hopkins to lend me the scarf pin," he informed me. " Maybe I can ask Jim Aldridge to return it to this Chinaman or possibly even to his mysterious master. I feel that Jim will be a more credible source for the object than would I, even should I disguise myself."

" And if it is accepted ?"

" Then I will be waiting, together with you, and with Hopkins and his minions, and we will put an end to this pilfering. We may never recover the stolen goods, but there is an excellent chance that we can put an end to this whole business."

We changed the direction of our course to take us to Scotland Yard, where Holmes explained our discoveries to Hopkins, who heard him in silence.

" It is a fine theory, Mr. Holmes," he said at length. " It would certainly appear to meet the facts of the case. The method of carrying the stolen articles out of the house is an ingenious one, to be sure. What did you make of the Chinaman, Doctor ?" he asked, suddenly turning to me.

" I am not sure what you expect me to say about him, though I noticed he was of below average height, slightly built, and had a scar stretching from the left corner of his mouth, going down along his chin." I fancied Holmes shot me an appreciative glance at this point, but I could not be certain.

" Did he, indeed ? Then I think we are talking of the 'Green Dragon', as he was known to the authorities in Hong Kong."

Holmes nodded. " I have heard of him. His real name is Dao Teng Tan, and he was one of the leaders of the most ruthless Tongs, or gangs, in that region. According to my sources, he has been personally responsible for the deaths of over thirty men at his hands. He is an extremely dangerous and wily opponent."

" What is he doing in London ?" I asked.

" He was forced to leave China following a dispute with another gang over opium dealings, in the course of which he suffered the injury that produced the scar you remarked, Watson. However, his whereabouts after leaving China were unknown, until now. I confess that although I knew of the Green Dragon's existence, I had not thought of associating him with the Chinaman we met just now until you mentioned him, Hopkins. My thanks."

Hopkins accepted the rare compliment with good grace. " It would be a feather in our caps, would it not, Mr. Holmes, if we were to put him behind bars ?"

" A feather in your cap, Hopkins," Holmes corrected him. " I feel that any credit should be yours rather than mine."

" Can we assume that he is the leader of this enterprise ?" I asked Holmes.

" I have little doubt of it. He is reported to be intelligent and cunning, and I am sure that he is not the sort to take orders from another in affairs of this kind. Yes, I think we may assume that he is the leader." Holmes stood silently, his head bowed, seemingly in thought. " Yes !" he exclaimed. " I think I may have it ! Hopkins, my apologies. I will contact you later. In the meantime, you may seek out Aldridge at this address," he scribbled a note on a page torn from his notebook. " Watson, come. I believe we have no time to waste."

We returned to Baker-street, where Holmes set me to work, researching the histories of those whose houses had suffered from the spate of losses, using the most recent edition of *Who's Who*, *Burke's*, and *Debrett's*. He himself disappeared on an undisclosed errand, returning in about an hour's time, as he had informed me that he would do.

" As I had thought," he exclaimed, flinging his hat into the corner with an air of impatience. " I am convinced that the name of the Green Dragon Line, whose ships ply between here and the Orient, is more than mere coincidence, but I am unable to discover any link between it and our quarry as the result of my searches at Lloyd's. I trust you have been more successful ?"

" Indeed I have," I was able to assure him. " Of those who have suffered losses, all have some connection with the East, specifically Hong Kong. Some held diplomatic posts there, some served with the Navy or the Army, and some worked in trading houses there."

" Excellent !" exclaimed Holmes. " I am certain that if we are to examine the composition of these households, we will find at least one servant in each who hails from China."

" When I was interviewing the housekeepers," I told him, " I observed an Oriental domestic in at least two of the houses. I have little doubt that you are correct in your supposition there."

While I was speaking, Holmes had picked up the morning paper, and was perusing it, while seemingly still attending to my words. " Aha !" he exclaimed. " I see here that the Eastern Pearl, of the Green Dragon Line is scheduled to sail for Hong Kong this very evening. We may well expect Dao Teng Tan to be on it. I fear that our sudden appearance at his door earlier may have forced his hand."

" You mean that he will take his loot and run ?" I asked.

" Precisely. We must get the pin to Aldridge, and thereby tempt Tan out of his lair."

Holmes sent a message to Scotland Yard, requesting Hopkins's urgent attendance at Baker-street, after first dispatching Billy to an address in the East End where Holmes assured him that he would find Aldridge.

Hopkins had been with us for less than twenty minutes when Aldridge was shown up to our room.

" I'm not in trouble, am I, Inspector ?" he asked, a frown corrugating his hideously scarred face as he recognised the police agent.

" By no means," Hopkins assured him. " We simply wish you to return the pin you found to one who will welcome its return. You can write, I take it ?"

" I'm no great shakes with a pen, but I can manage."

" Then write down that you have the pin, and you will hand it over, for a consideration – shall we say fifteen pounds, to the person to whom the message is addressed, at a place convenient to both of you. Shall we say the public bar of the George and Dragon in Limehouse at six this evening ? You know it ?" Holmes said to him. " Here is a pen, and here paper."

" I know the place. And who shall I address it to ?" asked the big man as he wrote, the tip of his tongue protruding from between his lips as he concentrated on his task.

" Never you mind. We will take care of the delivery. Ah, Wiggins," said Holmes, as the little urchin, whom Holmes had previously summoned, entered. " Take a good look at this man," indicating Aldridge. " I would like you to be able to describe him to others."

" Very good, sir," said Wiggins.

" And now, take this piece of paper, and make sure that you give it to the Chinaman you will find living at the Eastside Laundry at this address. Make sure that he knows that our friend here gave it to you. On no account are you to mention my name, nor that of Watson or Hopkins here."

" And this gentleman's name ?" asked Wiggins, looking at Aldridge.

" You do not know it and you have no need to know

it. Simply describe him to the Chinaman," Holmes told him. " Now, Hopkins," he said to the police agent after Wiggins had departed on his errand, and Aldridge, bearing the scarf-pin, on his, " we will need a good few of your constables stationed around the area. It is quite likely that the Green Dragon will be accompanied, and it would be advisable for us to scoop up the whole gang in the net."

" Indeed so," said Hopkins. " I will depart for Scotland Yard and issue the appropriate orders. You believe that this Aldridge will not fail us ?"

" I am certain of him," Holmes answered simply. " Slow of wit he may be, and uncouth of appearance, but Jim Aldridge has always been a man of his word and has fought fair, even when his opponents have not. Let us meet opposite the George and Dragon some fifteen minutes before the appointed time. You will, of course, ensure that no uniformed constables are in view of the place ?"

" Naturally," answered Hopkins. " We do not want to scare the game, do we ?"

" Indeed we do not."

" Well, Mr. Holmes, I must thank you for your assistance."

" And that of Aldridge, of course," I added.

" Indeed. Without him, we would be still racking our brains to discover the culprits involved in this case." With that, Hopkins took his leave of us.

" I believe Hopkins feels some excitement with regard to our little adventure," Holmes said to me, when we were alone together. " He has the makings of an excellent police officer were he to use his imagination a little more freely. As it is, his tenacity and his devotion to his duty are almost unsurpassed in the Metropolitan Police, and he shows more flashes of inspiration on occasion than one might expect by mere chance. As for us, Watson, I think we can trust to the forces of the Law on this occasion, and will not trouble to arm ourselves. Let us give Hopkins and his minions full credit for everything from now on. There is time, I believe, for us to take in the final movement of the symphony being performed at the Masons' Hall."

It was typical of Holmes that, even in the midst of a case such as this, which was rapidly reaching its climax, that he was seemingly able to immerse himself totally in the complexities and grandeur of Beethoven's noble music. At the end of the piece, as the applause grew, he turned to me with a smile.

" Now confess, Watson, even you were surely moved by that ?"

" I was, I admit it," I said, though in truth the majority of my thoughts had been running ahead, to the capture and arrest of the Green Dragon.

" Excellent – I am now in the mood for a spot of enjoyment. To the George and Dragon, then."

" Did you," I could not help enquiring, " choose that location at random ? The name seems somewhat appropriate."

He chuckled. " I confess that the irony of the name did appeal to me."

We met Hopkins, who was bundled up with a muffler covering most of his face. " I am known to half the villains of this area," he explained, " and I have no wish to advertise my presence on this occasion more than is necessary."

" Has Aldridge entered ?" Holmes asked him.

" He entered some two minutes or so before you arrived. He did not appear to notice me."

" Then you may depend upon it that he did not. Jim Aldridge's skills, such as they are, do not extend to dissimulation."

We waited in near-silence, Holmes softly humming the theme of the piece we had just heard, when Hopkins grasped my arm. " Is this him, Doctor ?" he asked, indicating a furtive figure making its way on the opposite side of the road.

I strained my eyes to discern any features, but was unable to do so, and said as much to Hopkins. " However," I added, " this man would seem to be smaller than the man who opened the door to us."

Our intended quarry entered the public house, and we waited in silence for a few minutes. Hopkins had removed his police whistle from his pocket, and stood, poised to blow a blast on it as soon as the opportunity presented itself.

" You do not propose to take him while he is inside ?" Holmes asked softly.

" No, we will wait till he is outside, with the goods on him."

Holmes nodded in silent agreement. " Ah, here he is, if I am not mistaken !"

Hopkins raised the whistle to his lips and blew a piercing blast. Instantly, several uniformed constables appeared, as if from nowhere, and flung themselves on the hapless individual hurrying along the street, before bringing him to the group of Hopkins, Holmes and myself.

" Well, my man, and what have you to say for yourself ?"

I looked at the Chinaman, who by now had ceased his struggles in the policemen's grip, and gasped.

" It is not he !" I exclaimed. " This is not the man who opened the door to us. This is not the Green Dragon !"

At this juncture, we were joined by Aldridge, who came out of the door of the inn, gesticulating.

" I have the pin, Mr. 'Olmes," he called. " This yeller beggar here wouldn't give me no money for it."

" Thank you, Jim," Holmes said. He turned to our captive. " Who are you ? Where is Tan ?"

" Tan gone," said the Chinaman in English that was barely comprehensible. " He go to China with big boat. All-all things he take with him."

" What ? When ?"

" One minute, one hour, two hour maybe. I not know."

" Where ?" asked Hopkins, in an agony of frustration.

" I not know. River I think. He not say," wailed our prisoner.

" Does he really not speak English ?" I asked.

" He hardly said a bloomin' word to me," put in Aldridge. " I showed him the pin and he tried to take it off me, but I soon put a stop to that. After that, he went all quiet like, until he suddenly got up and walked out on me. I waited a minute before I followed him, and saw you gents with him."

" Thank you, Jim," Holmes told him. " You have been most helpful."

" And the reward ?"

" I will pay you ten pounds myself," Holmes informed him, counting out ten sovereigns and passing them to Aldridge, who thanked him profusely. " Inspector, and Watson here, I ask you both to bear witness to the fact that I have advanced the reward for the recovery of the pin from my own pocket."

" Very good, Mr. Holmes," answered Hopkins. " I will ensure that you are repaid, never fear."

Holmes had been standing, brow furrowed in thought. " Come," he shouted to Hopkins and me. " There will be no time to lose ! The tide is on the turn !"

Hopkins and I looked at each other, and followed Holmes as he raced down the alleyway that led to the Thames.

At the water's edge, Holmes stopped, and pointed to a steamer to which a small boat was tied, with a figure climbing a rope ladder to board the bigger ship. The green dragon of the line was clearly visible against the black painted funnel.

" There is no smoke coming from her," Holmes exclaimed. " There may yet be time before she makes steam and gets under way."

Hopkins hailed a passing skiff, which he commandeered by the simple expedient of showing his police card to the astonished boatman, who undertook to ferry us to the ship.

" Ahoy !" shouted Holmes as we approached the vessel. " We are police. We are coming aboard."

A black-bearded European face, topped by a ship's officer's cap, appeared over the rail. " What do you want ?" was shouted down to us, in a strong Continental accent.

" By Jove !" exclaimed Holmes. " I know that face, do I not ? And so do you, Inspector, if I am not mistaken."

" Count Fyderyk Sliboffsky, the Polish navigator, adventurer and explorer, is it not ?" I interjected.

" Perfectly correct, Watson," Holmes confirmed. " The explorer of the Southern Seas and the Eastern Deserts, who recently mounted an expedition to locate the lost treasure of the Khans. I feel he may have fallen on hard times if he is being employed as an errand boy for the Green Dragon."

" There were always tales that his expeditions were no more than covers for smuggling adventures carried out at the request of others," said Hopkins. " This would seem to confirm those stories." He shouted up to the Pole. " We are coming aboard. Do not attempt to prevent us, or you will be arrested, and your ship impounded." He started up the rope ladder.

Holmes turned to me and chuckled quietly. " Hopkins is a true British bulldog when his blood is up, is he not ?" With that, he turned to the ladder and started to climb. I followed, after requesting our boatman to keep close to the ship, and slipping him a sovereign to ensure that he kept his word.

At the top of the ladder, I encountered Hopkins and Holmes, facing Sliboffsky, whom I could now perceive was wearing a captain's hat, and other items identifying him as the skipper of the vessel.

" You have no right !" the Pole was saying angrily to Hopkins. " It is my business and mine alone who travels on my ship, and the English police have no business here."

" On the contrary, my dear Count," replied Holmes in lazy tones. " This ship is in British waters, subject to British laws, and the British police have every right in the world to search this ship, especially as we have reason to believe that the results of several crimes are on board here."

The other shrugged. " As you will, but I would have you know that to the best of my knowledge, there is nothing on board this ship that can connect me to any wrong-doing."

" Who is the passenger who came aboard just now ?"

" Ah, the Chinaman ? A certain Sun Yee Chen, he tells me. A merchant who has been doing business in London, and now wishes to return to his native Canton."

" Would it surprise you," Hopkins asked him, " to learn that he is in fact the owner of the line of ships to which this vessel belongs, and he is a leader of criminal gangs in Hong Kong ?"

The explorer faced Hopkins defiantly. " I take my passengers at their word," he blustered. " I would advise you to do the same."

I grabbed Holmes' arm. " Look," I cried, pointing to the ship's funnel, out of which black smoke was now issuing.

" Yes," laughed the Pole. " You may be correct, Sherlock Holmes, but we will be under way in a matter of minutes, and you will be joining our little voyage." As he spoke, he produced a revolver from under his jacket, and pointed it at us. " Do not think of attacking me," he warned us, " or at least one of you will surely die."

As he spoke, I became conscious of a group of Lascars who appeared, seemingly from nowhere, and who surrounded us, with boathooks gripped menacingly in their hands, and looks of menace visible on their faces.

" Well," remarked Homes, with a bitter laugh, " it would seem that you currently hold a winning hand." It was with some surprise that I noted his seeming surrender to the facts of the situation. Hopkins, on the other hand, seemed to be bristling with indignation at this turn of events.

" What do you propose doing with us ?" he asked indignant-
ly. " Are we to become food for the fishes ?"

" Oh by no means," answered Sliboffsky. " As soon as we
are out of the sight of land, we will lower a boat and you will
be invited to take your leave of us. Or," and he paused to
stroke his beard, " it may be that we will save ourselves the
trouble of lowering the boat, and simply invite you to take
your leave without it. Maybe the fishes will feast. Maybe
they will not." He shrugged. " It is no concern of mine, the
appetite of the fishes."

" Who these ?" came a half-familiar voice from behind us,
and turning, I saw the Chinaman whom we had identified as
the Green Dragon.

" You do not recognise the famous Sherlock Holmes, and,
I presume, Doctor Watson ? The other is unknown to me,"
Sliboffsky answered him.

" Inspector Hopkins, Scotland Yard," the policeman identified himself. " I would advise you that you are committing
several felonies."

The Chinaman laughed unpleasantly. " No matter. You
die soon," he remarked in his broken English.

Holmes turned to face him. " In that case, I may as well
look my best," he smiled pleasantly, and to my surprise, withdrew the small mirror that he always carried with him, and
started to use it to assist him in the adjustment of his cravat.

The ship's siren blew. " We will be under way in a few
minutes," Sliboffsky informed us. " I will leave you, gentlemen. Make yourselves comfortable for the last hour
of your lives." He turned on his heel, leaving us with the
Chinaman, to whom he passed his revolver, and two of the
Lascars. Any thoughts that I might have had of overpower-
ing our captor were instantly quashed by the sight of the pistol in his hand and by the menacing stares of the Lascars. I
turned to Hopkins, and read a feeling of powerlessness in his

eyes. Holmes, for his part, seemed to be absorbed in achieving perfection in the tying of his cravat. At length he appeared to have finished his task, and turned to face Hopkins and me with what I would have sworn was a smile on his face, were it not for the circumstances.

The ship's siren blew once more, and I could hear the rattle of the anchor chains, and the shouts of the sailors as we set sail. I could see the London docks slipping past us as we moved downstream, and I resolved to meet my fate like an Englishman. The Chinaman's pistol never wavered as we passed the warehouses and wharves of the East End.

A voice hailed us from behind. " Ahoy, Eastern Pearl. Heave to or you will be fired upon !" The message was repeated, and Sliboffsky emerged from the wheelhouse, a megaphone in his hand. I turned to see from where the hail had originated, and saw a small steam-launch, with an officer of the River Police standing in the bow, a megaphone in his hand. Behind him knelt two policemen, armed with rifles.

" Heave to, I say !" came the call once more, but the Eastern Pearl continued on her course unabated. I could see the officer on the police launch turn and give orders to his two men, and in a short space of time I heard the distinctive cracks of two bullets fired from Lee-Metford rifles passing over our heads. The launch was now moving faster than the Pearl, and appeared to be manoeuvring to cut across our bows.

In order to avoid colliding with the launch, our helmsman was forced to turn sharply to port, and the ship heeled. Almost immediately, the bow of the Pearl ran aground on a mud bank, and the ship's deck lurched under our feet, throwing us all off balance. Holmes was the first to recover, and he ran at the Chinaman, knocking the revolver out of the other's hand, and almost in the same movement wrapping his arms round the other from behind, hereby immobilising him.

Hopkins and I quickly followed suit, and seized the two

Lascars. As we did so, two shots rang out from the police boat, and the windows of the wheelhouse shattered. Sliboffsky emerged from there, his hands raised, and the vibration from the engines died down.

We stood, waiting, while the police officer climbed up the Jacob's ladder at the side of the Pearl, followed by one of the riflemen, his weapon slung over his shoulder.

" Who signalled us with those flashes of light ?" asked the officer.

" It was I," replied Holmes.

" You are lucky that my sergeant here served in India and recognised the code that you used."

" I trusted that at least one of your men would possess that knowledge when I used my mirror to send my call for assistance. My compliments to you and your men on your speedy response. But now, do your duty, Inspector, and arrest these men." Holmes pointed to Sliboffsky and the Green Dragon, who appeared terrified at the sight of the rifle, now pointing in his direction. I picked up the revolver that he had dropped.

" And you are, sir ?" asked the inspector.

" My name is Sherlock Holmes, and here are Doctor Watson and Inspector Hopkins."

" I have heard your name, Mr. Holmes. Inspector, Doctor." He touched the brim of his cap in salute. " On what charges should we arrest these two ?" he asked Hopkins, but it was Holmes who answered.

" Abduction, smuggling, receiving stolen goods will suffice for a start. After that, you may find some murders and other lesser crimes will make themselves evident."

" Stolen goods ?" asked the visiting inspector.

" You will probably find a small box under this man's bunk in his cabin," Holmes told him, pointing to the Chinaman. " Count, perhaps you would be good enough to show Watson to the place ? And Watson, under no circumstances are you to open the box, but have the Count bring it here."

The inspector moved to the Chinaman, and used a pair of handcuffs that he removed from his pocket to pinion the other's hands behind his back.

Sliboffsky, after a glance at the revolver I was holding, sullenly led the way to a small cabin above the main deck, where he sullenly pointed to a small wooden box of obvious Oriental workmanship.

" Pick it up and walk ahead of me as we return to the others," I ordered him, reinforcing my words with the revolver.

Without warning, as we approached the doorway that led to the deck, Sliboffsky let out a piercing cry, and sank to the deck. I half-suspected a trick of some kind, but one look at his agonised face was sufficient to persuade me that this was no dissimulation on his part. As to the cause of his distress, it was not hard for me to find. The scoundrel had been furtively opening the box, no doubt with a view to abstracting some of the contents, but had been forestalled by the occupant of the box, which I now beheld as it writhed on the floor.

It was a gigantic centipede, somewhere in the region of a foot in length, with what I took to be jaws at one end, curved and pointed like fangs. I had only one thought – to destroy the brute – and accordingly I brought the heel of my boot down on the body of the loathsome thing, thereby dividing its body. The two parts writhed on the floor, but satisfied that the vile creature could not long live without a head, I bent to examine Sliboffsky, but a cursory examination was enough to tell me that his life would last only as long as that of the beast that had taken his own. Indeed, by the time I had picked up the box, after first gingerly assuring myself that no more of these venomous monstrosities lurked within, it was clear that life was extinct in both.

Holmes appeared astonished at the sight of me holding

the box, which bore obvious signs of its having been forced open. " My dear Watson," he exclaimed. " Did I not say to you that you were to leave the box untouched ? And where is Sliboffsky ?"

" He is dead," I told him, and explained the circumstances.

" Our friend here obviously decided this little pet – Vietnamese giant centipede, from your description – would form the best insurance against prying eyes. I am sure that he had his own way of dealing with the beast when the time came to open the box. Or maybe he was intending to leave the box unopened until the ship reached China, in which case, the thing would have perished of hunger," Holmes remarked. Meanwhile, the Green Dragon listened to all this with a smile on his face that I can only describe as diabolical. As Holmes came to the end of his explanation of the events, he gave a strange, almost unearthly, cry that froze the blood in my veins, and with a desperate wriggle and lunge, he leaped over the side of the ship. With his hands cuffed behind his back, there was no possibility of his being able to swim to shore, and it was certain that he must drown, but such is the force of self-preservation in human beings that he trod water, keeping his face, turned to the heavens, above the surface.

" Shall I go in after him, sir ?" the policeman asked his inspector, but it was Holmes who answered.

" You will save the taxpayer the cost of a hangman's rope if you let events run their natural course," he said. Hopkins nodded in silent agreement, and we watched, not without some pity on my part, the wretch's struggles in the water grow steadily weaker. His head sank, once, twice, three times, below the surface. The first two times, he rose to the surface again, but the third time, he failed to emerge, and we could see his body below us, half hidden by the water as it was swept away by the current.

" Very well, sir," said the inspector, with what sounded like a sigh of relief, wiping his brow. " And what, if I may ask, is in that box ?"

Holmes opened it, and displayed a mass of trinkets and baubles that, even to my inexpert eye, spoke of wealth and luxury.

" I recognise many of these from their description," said Hopkins. " That is the brooch reported missing by the Marchioness of Dundee, and the Earl of Ludlow's cufflinks."

" All small, unique of their kind, and thereby almost priceless" said Holmes. " They would fetch a pretty penny on the market. I am certain that once they had reached Hong Kong, our late friend would have attempted to 'fence' them in the United States, where the Chinese gangs have obtained a firm foothold."

" You have saved the reputation of the Force, Mr. Holmes," said Hopkins.

" My pleasure," answered Holmes, " but in this case, you may also thank Watson here, who has provided invaluable assistance."

" I only did what I could," I protested.

" It was enough," Holmes assured me. " A simple enough case, maybe, but one where your assistance was invaluable." Such praise, from one who did not often bestow it, and in the presence of others, was music to my ears, and helped me to forget the dangers and perils that we had recently encountered.

THE ADVENTURE
OF JOHN VINCENT
HARDEN

In The Adventure of the Solitary Cyclist, *Watson refers to Holmes being immersed in "...a very abstruse and complicated problem concerning the peculiar persecution to which John Vincent Harden, the well-known tobacco millionaire, had been subjected". No other details are provided, and we are left to judge for ourselves the complexity of the problem, as well as the nature of the persecution. Now this adventure of Sherlock Holmes has been discovered, and the truth is stranger than the tantalising glimpse given in Watson's notes.*

Some readers unfamiliar with the British peerage may be confused by the titles of Harden's wife. The daughter of a Duke is not herself a peeress, but is entitled to a courtesy title and is addressed as "Lady" followed by her Christian name. Upon marriage to a commoner, she may retain the courtesy title, consisting of "Lady" followed by her Christian name and her husband's surname. He acquires no title through the alliance.

T was a rare occasion on which I was able to add to my friend's knowledge of the world. I have in mind one such instance, which led to a case that proved to be among the more interesting of those undertaken by Sherlock Holmes. We were proceeding together along Regent-street, when Holmes' eye was caught by a crowd of street urchins surrounding a well-dressed man, who appeared to be frantically attempting to escape their attention.

" Halloa," exclaimed Holmes. " I wonder who that might be, and why he has attracted such unwelcome notice."

It gave me some satisfaction to be able to provide him with an answer. " The gentleman in question is John Vincent Harden, and he is by birth a native of Virginia in the United

States, though he now resides in this country, and he has amassed a fortune in tobacco."

Holmes regarded me quizzically. " How do you come to know him ?" he asked. " I recognise the name, but I confess to having had no idea as to Harden's appearance."

I laughed. " His marriage to Lady Julia, the daughter of the Duke of Northampton, was the social event of the year. The photographs of the young dashing millionaire and his beauteous bride were in all the illustrated magazines."

My friend shook his head. " Were they indeed ? The whole affair passed me by unnoticed. But what is going on ?" There were sounds of raised voices, the shriller voices of the street Arabs, and a deeper tone, which I took to be that of Harden. The voices suddenly stilled as the sound of a police whistle rent the air, and a uniformed constable pushed his way through the boys towards the beleaguered man, who, even as I watched, turned pale and dropped, apparently senseless, to the ground.

Immediately, I made my way forward. By good chance, I happened to have with me my medical bag, having attended a case immediately before meeting Holmes, and, introducing myself to the constable as a member of the medical profession, bent to render aid to the stricken man.

Upon my administering some sal volatile under his nose, he stirred a little and opened his eyes.

" Are they gone ?" he asked me.

I took it that he was referring to the boys who had been persecuting him, and looked around. It seemed that the policeman had succeeded in dispersing his tormentors, and I informed him of the fact, together with my qualifications as a doctor.

" Excellent," he replied, in a voice that had but little of the American about it. " I apologise for my weakness, but this has been a strain under which I have lived for the past few months. I fear that my nerves will not permit me to venture outside my home if this continues."

" This is not a new complaint, then ?" I enquired.

" By no means. This dreadful business has been going on for some time, and I am at my wits' end to know it might cease."

" This would appear to be a case for my friend," I told him. I looked around for Holmes, but he was nowhere to be seen. " Come with me," I said to my patient, helping him to his feet, and hailing a hansom, which I directed to take us to Baker-street.

On arrival at 221B, I opened the door to our rooms to discover Holmes already there, reclining in his usual chair, and drawing contentedly on his pipe.

" I had guessed that you would be bringing Mr. Harden here," he smiled, " and therefore made my way here to arrange that Mrs. Hudson should bring us some refreshment. I trust that Watson here has taken good care of you ?" he asked Harden.

" Why, yes, indeed," replied our visitor, somewhat bemused. " May I ask whom I have the honour of addressing ? You are a doctor ?"

Holmes' eyebrows raised somewhat. " Ah, Watson failed to provide my name ? I am Sherlock Holmes."

" The detective ? Your fame, Mr. Holmes, has crossed the oceans. Even a lowly American-born boy like myself has heard of your adventures."

" Lowly ?" Holmes responded. " Quite apart from your marriage to the daughter of one of the oldest families of England, you have acquired somewhat of a reputation in your own right, if my sources are correct, with regard to your wealth and your singular methods of disposing of it."

" Ah, you refer to my habits prior to my marriage ? Yes, I

confess that my addiction to gambling, and placing wagers of all kinds was somewhat out of the ordinary."

" The occasion on which you wagered ten thousand dollars on which of two ducks would first step onto the opposite bank of a river, for example ?"

" Five thousand only, sir. The tale grew in the telling. But I am now a married man, with a married man's responsibilities. My father-in-law, the Duke, has warned me that he wishes to hear no more of such tales, and I, happy in my marriage, am content to give him assurance that he never will."

" And yet, what is the meaning of today's incident ?" I asked.

He sighed. " As I mentioned to you, Doctor Watson, I have been the target of abuse and torment at the hands of these little ruffians for some time now. I had believed myself to be safe in the area of Regent-street, but these imps followed me from my house near the Park to Regent-street, shouting and abusing me all the way."

" I could not distinguish the words," Holmes told him. " What manner of abuse was this ?"

" Chiefly demands for money," our visitor replied with a blush. " And there were other matters referred to, of a personal nature."

Holmes said nothing, but raised his eyebrows slightly.

" I guess I should explain," said Harden. " I am, as you are probably aware, a wealthy man, as these things are reckoned. As such, in America, where wealth and not birth alone is a passport to the best societies, I was moving in exalted circles."

Holmes smiled. " Despite all that you may have heard of the British, the truth, when one examines it, is not very different from that of America. But pray, continue."

" As I previously said to you, I was addicted to

gambling. One evening, when I was somewhat in liquor, as I believe you say in this country, I made a shameful wager."

" Shameful in what sense ?"

" It concerned the daughter of a prominent man of the district. I would prefer not go into the details, but I would say that it involved some acts of an intimate nature between me and this woman. I won my wager, I am sorry to say, and I am ashamed of what I did, both of the infamous act itself, and the fact that I made a wager concerning it."

" And this is somehow connected with the persecution you are currently experiencing at the hands of these street urchins ?"

" It is most closely connected."

" The name of the man whose daughter was involved in this business ?"

" I would prefer not to mention it. Let me just say that he has risen to be a national figure, first as one of the United States Senators from our state, and lately has taken a place in the national Cabinet."

Holmes said nothing, but scribbled a name in his notebook, tore out the page, and handed it to Harden, who nodded. " You are correct, Mr. Holmes. It is he."

" He would seem to be a dangerous man to have as an enemy."

" And yet, when I lived in America, I met him many times, and there was no sense of animosity. He hardly appeared to me as an enemy at that time."

" It would appear, then, that he only discovered your adventure, if I may term it so, following your arrival in this country. Always assuming, that it, that it is he who is responsible for all of this."

" Who else could it be who would do such a thing ? It was certainly after I arrived here, but it was some time following my marriage that the persecution started. I tell you,

Mr. Holmes, it is going to be my undoing. I have to tell you that I bitterly regret my action. Indeed, within two days of winning the wager, I returned the money I had won, telling the other that I could not accept it. Poor fellow, he was not long for this life after my action, but it gave me some peace of mind. And now... now this."

" Surely the taunts of a few street Arabs cannot mean so much ?"

" If it were only that, Mr. Holmes, I would not say that I would be a happy man, but I would be much more at ease."

" There is more ?"

" Obscene and disgusting letters appear on my desk in the study of our London house. They have not passed through the hands of the Post Office. They are unstamped and placed in pristine envelopes."

" Then one of the servants has placed them there, evidently."

" Evidently. But which of them has done this ? I have asked them all if they have placed anything on my desk. Of course, I do not mention what it is about which I am making the enquiry. However, none of them admits to anything. And, Mr. Holmes," and here Harden spread his hands in a gesture of helplessness, " I am a prisoner of your culture. I am a plain-speaking American and, forgive me, I find your English ways to be somewhat circuitous, and maybe even devious. I find myself unable to judge whether the servants are telling the truth or not. All have come highly recommended, and most have been in the service of Julia's family for many years."

" And naturally, you cannot tell your wife any of this. I understand that. What is the content of these letters ?"

Again, Harden blushed. " They are such as I would not care to repeat anywhere. They make explicit reference to the wager that I made concerning Annabel – that is to say, the politician's daughter."

" And yet few would know of it ?"

" Very few people knew of this wager. The man with whom I made the wager and two others who were present when the wager was made and acted as witnesses. None of these is in this country, and indeed, one of the witnesses is no longer on this earth, having died some years ago."

" And apart from these references to your past, what more is contained in these messages ? Demands for money, perhaps ?"

Harden shook his head. " Nothing of that nature. I confess to having expected some sort of blackmail when I saw the first of these letters."

" Would it be possible to see one of them ?"

" You may see for yourself," Harden answered him, reaching in his coat pocket. " I cannot leave these letters lying around the house where Julia might chance upon them."

" And you choose not to destroy them ?"

" I cannot, Mr. Holmes. They serve me as a reminder of my determination never to return to the past – to be the man I once was." He handed a folded piece of paper to Holmes, who examined it through one of his powerful lenses.

" The paper itself is unremarkable, such as may be purchased at any stationer's in London. The ink is Indian ink. I take it you keep none such in your house ?"

" There might be some used by the servants for marking items of laundry, I guess, but to the best of my knowledge, the answer to your question is a negative."

Holmes bent to the paper again. " The handwriting is definitely masculine, and almost certainly disguised. As to the matter of this missive—" Holmes shrugged. " I refrain from passing comment. I take it that what is described here is an accurate account of what occurred ?" The scarlet-faced Harden nodded dumbly. " And this is the kind of matter that the street urchins have been shouting after you ?"

" Their taunts have been similar, yes, but somewhat less explicit."

Holmes refolded the paper and passed it back to Harden, who put it in his pocket. " If I may be permitted to offer a little advice," he said to our visitor, " I would immediately refrain from keeping them upon my person. Why, suppose it had been someone other than Watson who had assisted you, and had discovered those papers in your pocket ? Someone with fewer scruples than my friend here ?"

A look of horror spread over Harden's face as the possible consequences became obvious to him. " You are perfectly right, Mr. Holmes," he said, and withdrew them. He appeared to be about to cast them into the fire, when Holmes held out his hand.

" Pray allow me to keep them safe," he said. " They are evidence, though naturally, I would never dream of exhibiting them in public, and they may prove to be a valuable weapon in the fight against your tormentors."

Harden's face cleared. " You will act for me in this business, then ?" he exclaimed, with an evident air of relief.

" My dear sir, I had taken it for granted that you would wish me to do so," smiled Holmes.

" Please allow me to give you my card," said Harden. " Should you discover anything of interest, you will let me know ?"

" Naturally," said Holmes. " And I will expect you to play your part, by keeping me informed of any further developments at your end."

When Harden had left, Holmes, as was his habit, turned to me. " Well, Watson, what do you make of this ?"

" I hardly know what to say. I can see little motive for this persecution, other than that Mr. Harden would appear to be a somewhat sensitive young man, somewhat removed from the idea of the rough and tumble American that we are accustomed to imagining."

" 'Sensitive', indeed," said Holmes. " The very word. And I, too, wonder at the motives for such a persecution. Without a demand for money, or anything similar, it is hard to imagine what the aims of the criminal writing these notes, and paying the urchins to harass him, might be. I believe this is a case for Wiggins and the Baker-street Irregulars." He rang the bell, and gave orders to Billy, our page, to locate Wiggins and bring him to 221B. " In the meantime," he added, addressing me, " perhaps you can furnish me with a diagnosis of your patient."

" It is hard to tell, but when I examined him in the street, his heartbeat seemed irregular – perhaps more so than I would expect from a young man, even given the circumstances under which I found him. Also, as we have agreed, he appears overly nervous – I might even describe him as being mentally frail. Tell me, have you discovered anything more from the letters that he passed to you ?"

" I did not like to mention this before Harden, but it is my opinion that these letters proceed from no less a personage than Joshua Leman. I see the name means little to you. You may recall that at the time when we were dealing with Sir Henry Baskerville and his canine troubles, I informed you that I was engaged in a case concerning the blackmail of a prominent member of Society. My opponent on that occasion was Leman, and he proved a foe worthy of my steel. He, like Harden, originated on the far side of the Atlantic, and made his way to our shores. In Leman's case, however, it was not love that brought him hither, I am sure, but fear of arrest and conviction were he to remain in his native land for any extended period."

" And you feel that this is his work ?"

" The writing is close to what I have encountered earlier,

and the use of Indian ink as the medium in which the note is written is also most distinctive. If it were accompanied by demands for money, I would be almost certain of its authorship. However, since no such demand has been received, I confess I am baffled."

" But how have these documents arrived on his desk, given that the servants all protest their innocence ?"

" Leman's tools are the servants of his victims. They are his eyes and ears, reporting to him all that may be of interest to him with regard to their masters and mistresses. On occasion, as I suspect is the case in this instance, they act as his hands, working his will at a distance. It is this that makes it so deucedly hard to prove anything against him. This may indeed prove to be one case where the wiles of the old country have overcome the naive optimism of the young colonial."

Shortly after this exchange, Mrs. Hudson admitted Wiggins, who reported to Holmes with the solemnity of a subaltern reporting to his colonel.

" There is a gentleman living at this address," Holmes told the lad, giving him the street and number of Harden's house. " He is being followed around London by a group of boys who are shouting at him."

" Shouting what sort of things, sir ?"

" I want you to find out exactly what they are being told to shout, and who is telling them to insult this gentleman. You may carry this out alone, or you may choose to involve some of the other Irregulars. It is your choice. If you can come back to me by this time tomorrow with the answers to these questions, I will be most pleased, and I will pay you handsomely. Here are two shillings on account."

" Thank you, sir," said Wiggins, touching his cap. " I'll get you your answers, never fear, sir."

" If that lad had had the benefit of being born into a better family, he would have the chance of becoming one of Scotland

Yard's finest officers when he grows up," Holmes remarked to me as the sound of Wiggins' boots down the stairs faded. " As it is, when he is of a proper age, I intend recommending him to one of the more intelligent of the Scotland Yarders – perhaps Hopkins – with the strong recommendation that his background, such as it is, be ignored, and his intelligence and initiative, which are considerable, be nurtured and encouraged."

 T was with an air of great confidence that Holmes uttered these words regarding the source of Harden's letters that I have recorded above, and it was with some surprise that he was proved wrong the very next morning, by the arrival of Harden at Baker-street, brandishing a piece of paper.

" Another one ?" Holmes asked.

" Indeed. It appeared on my desk some time last night. I discovered it this morning."

" I see," said Holmes.

" I perceive that you are unimpressed by this, sir. Let me tell you more, which I omitted to tell you yesterday. My desk is of the roll-top type, where the surface of the desk is hidden by a sliding cover. In the past, I did not lock the cover at night, but since the first letter appeared on the desk, I started to secure the desk before retiring, and the letters still appeared beneath the locked cover."

" And this letter that appeared today ?"

" Was found by me when I unlocked the desk this morning."

" I assume that you hold the only key ?"

" This key here on my watch-chain. To the best of my knowledge, there is no other."

Holmes requested that he be allowed to examine it closely, and, having received it from Harden, proceeded to scrutinise it through his lens. Having done so, he thanked Harden and returned it to him.

" Do you not wish to see the letter ?" Harden asked, and passed the paper, in its turn, to Holmes, who read through it.

" There would appear to be some sort of implied threat here," said Holmes. " Nothing explicit, but it seems to me that there is more than a hint that you should divorce your wife and return to America."

" That is precisely what those wretched boys told me as I was coming here."

" Then there is a definite link between the urchins and these letters. Not that I ever doubted that there was such a link, but this is proof positive. I have a spy in their ranks, however, and I hope to be able to tell you more about the origin of these letters shortly. For now, may I ask you to continue walking and showing yourself as much as possible. I sincerely believe that you are in no danger from these boys, though I appreciate that it is uncomfortable, or even painful, for you to expose yourself to their gibes. The more that you are mocked and persecuted, the more we will learn about those who are inflicting this upon you."

Harden sighed. " I will do as you request, Mr. Holmes, though as you say, it will be more than uncomfortable for me."

He left us, and Holmes leaped up from his chair. " We must act soon," he said. " I fear the end-game is close at hand. The pawns have moved, and cleared the way for the more powerful pieces on the board."

" Why, whatever can you mean ?" I asked. " Where are we going ?"

" Our first call will be at the back door of Harden's house. Come." He seized his hat and stick and swept out of the room, and I followed in his wake.

We took a somewhat circuitous route to the Park, presumably to avoid Harden, and we were soon knocking at the kitchen door below the area steps, which was opened to us by a kitchen-maid, who stared at us with a look of astonishment on her face.

" If it's the master or the mistress that you're wanting, then the door's upstairs, and it's one of the men who'll be opening it to you, not me."

" My dear young lady," Holmes answered her with his most winning smile, " it is the housekeeper with whom we wish to speak. If you would be so kind as to let her know that we await the pleasure of her company, I would be most grateful." I observed a shilling change hands, and the maid disappeared in search of the housekeeper, who appeared some minutes later, introducing herself as Mrs. Bulstrode.

" I am not sure, I must say, what a gentleman like you wants with me," she offered.

" It is a mere trifle, madam," Holmes answered her. " I merely wish to know the name of the locksmith with which this household deals. I am sure that a fine housekeeper such as yourself knows all the tradesmen with whom the house does business."

" That would be Albert Finchley, on the Tottenham Court-road, sir," she answered. " He's really an ironmonger, but he does a bit of locksmithing from time to time, and any time we need a new key or a lock fixed or something like that, we go to him." She suddenly seemed to become suspicious. " What do you want to know this sort of thing for ?" she asked.

Sherlock Holmes introduced himself.

" I've read of you in the papers," she said. " And you," turning to me, " must be Doctor Wilson."

" Watson," I corrected her.

" Well, Mr. Holmes, there's been no murders done here, so I'm sure I don't know what you're doing. I've a good mind to tell the mistress you've been here."

" Not the master ?" Holmes smiled.

" He's all right, I suppose," she admitted, " but I've been with Lady Julia's family since she was a girl."

" There are reasons why I would like my visit here kept quiet, but I am not at liberty right now to tell you what they are," Holmes said to her. " I will simply say that it concerns a personal matter that may cause some harm to your mistress if it is badly handled."

" I'll take your word for it, sir, but if there's any trouble, I know who you are and what you've been asking."

" One more question, if I may," said Holmes, holding up a finger. " What is the name of Lady Harden's lady's maid ?"

" Why, that would be Lucy Jones, who's also been with her since she was a little child."

" Thank you, that is most helpful," Holmes informed her, tipping his hat. " And now," as the area door closed, " we are for Mr. Finchley's emporium."

Albert Finchley's shop transpired to be typical of its kind, hung about with miscellaneous items, including a display of locks, and a notice informing customers that Mr. Finchley offered prompt and accurate key-cutting services.

My friend introduced himself to Finchley, and enquired if he was the supplier of any items to the Harden household.

" Why, yes. Mrs. Bulstrode, the housekeeper, has often sent orders to me, and I am happy to oblige. They pay good money, promptly, which is more than you can say for many nowadays."

" Your work for the house includes locksmith work ?"

The honest shopkeeper scratched his head as he searched his memory. " I can't say that I have ever fitted a lock there," he replied at length. " I've cut a few keys for the place, though."

" What was the last key you cut ?"

" Let me think. Yes, it was a small key, the sort you might use on a chest or a trunk. That was an odd one, though."

" Why do you say that ?"

" I wasn't cutting from a key, but from an impression of a key in red clay."

" When was this ?"

" About a week ago, I would say, sir."

" And who was the person with whom you dealt on this occasion."

" One of the maids. Pretty little thing. She game her name as Lucy, but I never did get her last name."

" That is most helpful, Mr. Finchley."

We returned to Baker-street. It was clear that Holmes had observed some items which had escaped my notice, but I was completely at a loss as to what they might be.

On our arrival at 221B, Mrs. Hudson informed us that Wiggins had arrived. " I didn't want to send him upstairs to your room, sir," she told Holmes, " so he's waiting in the kitchen with Cook."

" Send him up, Mrs. Hudson, send him up," replied Holmes, seemingly in excellent humour. " Well, Wiggins, what have you for me ?" he asked, when the leader of the Irregulars appeared, clutching his cap in his hands. " Sit in that chair, won't you ?"

" Thank you, sir," Wiggins answered. " I did it all myself," he said, with an air of some pride. " I went round to behind the house, and there was twenty lads there all waiting just round the corner. I asked them what they were waiting for, and they said it was for the man who was going to tell them what they should shout at the gentleman when he came out."

" I see," said Holmes. " And you offered to shout along with them ?"

" One of the lads who was there the day before had fallen sick, so there was a space for me, they said. I wasn't going to take any of their money away from them."

" What was the pay ?"

" Five shillings for the day, and there was twenty of them exactly. I counted them."

" Five pounds a day ?" I interjected. " Whoever is behind this has long pockets."

" I think we knew that already," Holmes said, a trifle impatiently. " Go on, Wiggins."

" Well, sir, this man came along. Gentleman, I should say, really, because he was a bit of a swell. He was a tall thin man, and spoke sort of funny. I think he was an American, but I couldn't be sure of that. He had a funny little moustache, and was dressed in a flash kind of way, with a large sparkling tie-pin."

" Excellent, Wiggins. Anything else ?"

" Yes, sir, his boots seemed a bit strange. They had pointed toes and shiny metal fittings on the toes."

" And what did this 'swell' have to say to you ?"

" He told us that we should shout that the gentleman should leave his wife and go back to America."

" Did he say why you were to do this ?"

" No, but one of the lads with me said that it was some trouble with another woman. Another said it was trouble with money. Sorry, sir, but I was unable to find out." Wiggins appeared a little dejected at his failure.

" Never mind, Wiggins, you have done excellently. Better than I had hoped. So you received your five shillings ?"

" I did, sir."

" And here are another five to go with them."

" Why, thank you, sir. Will you want me to join the group again tomorrow ?"

Holmes smiled. " I do not want to deprive you of your five shillings, but be warned that this opportunity of earning easy money will not continue for much longer. Please continue with the work. If you discover anything new, please let me know as soon as possible, but do not feel that you must continue with daily reports. Thank you, Wiggins."

I let Wiggins out of the house, and returned to Holmes, who was chuckling. " It is Leman, all right. Wiggins has given us an excellent description, down to the boots, which are of the type worn in the western part of the United States."

" And he has subverted the maid of the lady of the house to assist him in his nefarious schemes ?"

Holmes furrowed his brow. " I have yet to be wholly convinced of that," he said. " A few details seem to argue against that supposition."

" Then how did Lucy, the maid, come by the the impression of the key ? Are you suggesting that she removed the key from Harden's watch-chain and took the impression ? How would she be able to accomplish that ?"

" I do not believe that she removed the key or that she made the impression. She was given the clay containing the impression of the key, and orders to have a duplicate key to the desk cut."

" By Leman ?"

Holmes shook his head. " By another."

" But if not by Leman, by whom ? Another one of the household ?"

" I cannot be certain at present, but I have my suspicions. Much depends on the past history of the players in this little drama."

" Harden has told us of his part in all of this, has he not ?"

" He has told us what he considers to be relevant, yes, but in cases such as this, an observer from outside may be better placed to judge the relevancy of events. I believe there is more to this business than we have been told."

" And how do you propose to accomplish the discovery of this additional information ?"

" I believe you may be of great assistance here, Watson."

" I ?" I enquired incredulously.

" Yes, indeed. You were kind enough to inform me of Harden's identity the other day when we first encountered him. Your reading of those sections of the newspapers that I typically ignore may well prove to be a great benefit. For example, what were Lady Julia's romantic inclinations before she took up with Harden ? Were they ever reported by the Press ?"

" Yes, indeed. She was engaged, in fact, to another American, who died some time back. Now that I come to recall some of the details, he was from the same state as Harden."

" And perhaps moved in the same social circles ?" Holmes mused. " It is not without the bounds of possibility that they were acquainted. Watson, can you recall the name of Lady Julia's previous fiancé ?"

" If I remember correctly, it was a Mr. Jonathan Eddoes, whose father likewise owned tobacco plantations."

" We are drawing the threads together, Watson." Holmes rubbed his hands together, thereby signifying his satisfaction. " A few more answers from Mr. Harden, and I think it will be to our advantage to speak also with Lady Harden, and I believe we will then have all the answers."

" I am still in the dark," I confessed. " Although there would appear to be some connections, I cannot string them together into a connected whole."

" No matter," my friend told me. " All will become clear. I think we must talk once more with Mr. Harden." He dispatched Billy with a message to Harden, informing the latter that we would be calling upon him later that day.

N arrival at Harden's house, we were admitted by a footman. " Would it be possible," Holmes asked him, as he took our hats and sticks, " for me to speak briefly with the maid Lucy Jones before you tell Mr. Harden we are here ?"

The footman showed a little surprise at this request, but agreed to let us speak to the girl, who arrived, a little flushed and excited.

" I'm not in any trouble, am I, sir ?" she asked Holmes.

" By no means," he assured her. " You have been in Lady Julia's service for some time ?"

" I've been with the family since she was a babe in arms, sir."

" And you were acquainted with Mr. Eddoes, when she was engaged to that gentleman ?"

Her face took on a sad cast. " I was indeed, sir. He was a real gentleman, and I thought that Lady Julia's heart would break when he died of the fever that carried him off. She was lucky that Mr. Harden was such a good friend of Mr. Eddoes, and was able to help her forget him." She paused and appeared to collect herself. " Not that Mr. Harden isn't a gentleman in his own right, you understand, sir, but there was something about Mr. Eddoes that was kind of special, for all that he was an American."

" Thank you, Lucy." I saw some silver change hands. " You have been most helpful."

" This way, sirs." The footman, who had been standing at a discreet distance, ushered us into a room that was plainly the study.

" Aha ! We have the famed roll-top desk before us," Holmes exclaimed when the servant had retired. He whipped his ever-present lens from his pocket and bent to examine the lock. " A simple lock," he remarked. " Hardly worth going to the trouble of duplicating the key. Even an amateur such as myself could open this in seconds."

He had just straightened up, and returned the lens to his pocket when Harden entered.

" Any developments ?" he asked. " Is this urgent ? I am due at my Club in less than half an hour."

" It will not take long," Holmes told him, " but I felt it better to talk face to face. Firstly, I believe that you were acquainted with Mr. Jonathan Eddoes. Was he one of those who witnessed your wager ?"

" I knew him well. Indeed, he was the man with whom I made that infamous wager. You may be aware that he was engaged to be married to Lady Julia. When he died, it fell to me to console her for her loss."

" And the result of your consolation was your present marriage," Holmes remarked drily.

" What do you mean by that, sir ?" Harden's tone was indignant.

" There was no hidden meaning behind those words, Mr. Harden, I assure you. I have more questions. Have you ever been acquainted with a certain Joshua Leman ?"

At the mention of this name, Harden's face grew dark. " A rogue and a rascal. He was no friend of mine, though Jonathan – Eddoes, that is – had some acquaintance with him. I believed him to have cheated at cards, and refused to admit him to any gathering hosted by myself."

" Would he have known of the wager ?"

" Certainly I never informed him of it."

" One last question, which is somewhat personal, but I would be obliged if you could see your way to answering it. What are the financial terms of your marriage ?"

" I really think that is no business of yours, Mr. Holmes."

" I believe it to be very much my business. It is most germane to the problem currently at hand."

" Very well then. I am, as you are aware, possessed of considerable wealth. My wife brought no dowry with her – nothing except her good name. I may tell you in confidence that her family, though one of the oldest and most noble in the land, is in a state of penury."

" I was already aware of that fact," said Holmes, " though few others are."

" My money has helped to restore the family fortunes. As I mentioned in our previous conversation, His Grace her father is concerned about my history of gambling. One of the conditions of my marriage to his daughter was that, should the marriage at any time be dissolved, as he threatened it would be should I relapse into my previous bad habits, I would forfeit a large sum of money, to be given to Julia."

" I see," said Holmes simply. " Thank you very much for your frank answer."

" Will that be all ?"

" It is all," Holmes told him. " Again, my thanks."

We left the house, with Holmes in high good humour. " I have it all, now, Watson, other than one piece of the puzzle, which I expect to discover shortly."

" But if it is Leman, as seems evident, why are there no demands for money ?"

" He is playing a long game. Stop, and wait." He caught hold of my arm as we were about to turn the corner of the square where Harden's house was located. " Ha ! There he goes !" He indicated Harden, who set off at a brisk pace in the direction of Pall Mall. Almost instantly, a group of street boys, among whom I recognised Wiggins, clustered around him, clamouring loudly, though it was impossible to make out their words. " And now," he said, as the cortège swept around the corner, " for Lady Julia."

I was amazed at these words. " Why involve her ? She knows nothing about this matter."

" She knows more than you might imagine," he told me, ringing the bell once more. The door was opened by the same footman who had opened it to us previously, and who regarded us with an air of astonishment, as well he might, having let us out of the house not some five minutes previously.

" I appear to have forgotten my gloves," Holmes told him calmly. " No, do not trouble yourself. I know exactly where I left them, and I will retrieve them myself." So saying, he stepped into the hallway, and I followed. " And by the way," he called over his shoulder as he led the way to the study where we had previously talked with Harden, " please inform Lady Harden that Sherlock Holmes would like a word with her about the little matter of Joshua Leman."

Holmes, as I had suspected, had not left his gloves in the house, but it had allowed us entry, and we awaited Lady Harden. She entered the room, and I bowed as Holmes inclined his head. Her photographs had done her less than justice, and I found myself looking at one of the most beautiful women I have ever beheld. Her face, however, was set and pale.

" How do you come to know of Joshua Leman and my relationship with him ?" she asked in a cold tone, which failed to mask a thread of fear.

" It is, as I have said to others elsewhere at other times, my business to know what others do not," he replied calmly. " How much are you paying him ?"

I was astounded by this question, but my astonishment was nothing compared to that of Lady Harden, who sank, almost senseless, onto the sofa behind her. " How did you know ?"

" It was elementary," Holmes told her. " Leman always plays his foul tricks for financial gain. He is not asking your husband for any money, therefore he must be obtaining an income from another source. And you, Lady Julia, are that source."

" It would appear that I must tell you all, then," she said. There were tears in her eyes as she began her tale. " I knew Jonathan Eddoes from the time I first visited America as a child. Our families were more than happy that we should marry, and when he proposed marriage to me, I believed I was the happiest woman on earth. He had many friends, among them my present husband, whom I liked well enough. When Jonathan fell sick, I was heartbroken. I knew from the start that there was no recovery from the malady from which he was suffering, and I mourned his loss long before he was taken from me." Here she paused, and wiped her eyes with a lacy handkerchief. " Jonathan, noble soul that he was, could not bear to see me suffer, although he was in pain himself. He made John Harden promise to take care of me after— after he was gone, and made me promise not to repel any advances that he might make.

" I realised what my beloved Jonathan was doing for me, and though I liked Harden well enough, I knew that no-one could replace Jonathan in my heart. And now I come to the most terrible thing of all. Before Jonathan had passed away, Harden had asked for my hand in marriage,and I had accepted. Jonathan, with his typical generosity of spirit, had given his blessing to the nuptials, even though he knew he would not live to be present. The engagement was announced in all the newspapers. And then... then..." She appeared to lose her composure, and Holmes and I waited in silence while she regained it. " It was two nights before he died. He summoned me to his bedside, and he told me a terrible tale. Harden had made the most infamous wager that besmirched the honour of an innocent girl. He begged me to forget the matter, as far as was in my power."

" Why did he tell you this ?" Holmes broke in.

" He told me he was ashamed of his part in this wager, and he wished to cleanse himself of guilt before he died. However, following this revelation, I found myself unable to look upon Harden with the same affection that I had previously felt for him, nor have I ever been able to do so since then. It was expected, however, that we would be married – our betroth-al had been announced, and the wedding arrangements had been made. It would have caused a scandal if I had refused him. But what he had done was itself most shameful and scandalous. And indeed, it was with scandal in mind that the rogue Leman approached me shortly after our wedding. He was aware of the fact that the wager had been made – I be-lieve that my fiancé may have told him—" (" Aha !" exclaimed Holmes) " —and had somehow discovered that Jonathan had told me of it. I do not know how. Maybe he had visited my fiancé after I had been informed of this thing, and Jonathan had confessed to him that he had told me. I do not trust him," she added suddenly, and shuddered as she seemed to withdraw into herself.

" You are right not to trust him," Holmes told her. " He is a serpent of the worst kind, and it is an ambition of mine to silence his poisonous tongue for ever. Let me finish the story for you, and you will tell me if I am mistaken. Leman first proposed blackmailing your husband, but you saw a way of ridding yourself of a man you had come to despise, while en-suring your family's financial future. You paid him money for him to harass Harden in such a way that he would be forced to separate from you, or be separated by the order of your father, the Duke. Upon such a separation, you would receive a set-tlement – I have been informed of this by your husband. The harassment was to be done through the gibes of street urchins, and anonymous letters, written by Leman, and delivered to his desk by you. You had caused a duplicate key to be made – I am guessing that Leman instructed you as to the meth-od. Am I correct so far ?"

" Oh, Mr. Holmes, your reputation is well deserved. It is

as you say, save for one detail. Leman will receive his money following the separation. I have not yet paid him a penny."

" Nor will you ever need to," said Holmes. " I will put a stop to his antics at once, and you, Lady Julia, must also cease. Your husband does not strike me as an evil man. He appears to be genuinely remorseful regarding his past action. Has he told you, or did Eddoes inform you, that your husband repaid the amount of the wager within days of his receiving the money from Eddoes ? He did not ? I am certain that little detail would never come to your ears from Leman."

" You believe he is sorry for what he did ?"

" I cannot be completely certain of this, but it is my sincere belief that he bitterly regrets his life and his actions before he married you, Lady Julia."

" Mine also," I added.

Lady Harden bit her lip and frowned. " He is not a bad man or a bad husband when all is taken into consideration," she eventually answered in a quiet tone. " It is merely my pride that has kept me from him, and has spurred this business with Leman. If you can silence Leman, I will do my part to be a good wife to him."

" Thank you, Lady Julia," Holmes replied. " I believe Leman will bother you no more. I must ask you, however, if you would be prepared to swear in court to what you have just told us ?"

" I would," she said in a stronger tone. " Thank you, Mr. Holmes, for giving me hope, and removing this weight from me."

  have waited for some time for this," Holmes told me, as we sped through the streets in a hansom towards an address in South London, some days later. The time immediately following our conversation with Lady Julia Harden had been largely concerned with the events I have described under the title of " The Adventure of the Solitary Cyclist", but Holmes, with his usual energy, had at the same time been conducting his researches into the Harden case. " He has been under my eye almost since his arrival in this country," he said, referring to Joshua Leman, " but as yet, I have been unable to establish any proof of any criminal act. Lady Julia's testimony will not be needed, I am sure, but the mere threat of it may well be enough to put an end to his mischief."

We arrived at the street in Battersea where Holmes had directed the cab, and paid off the driver.

" Now for it," said Holmes, rapping smartly with the head of his cane at the door of one of the houses. It was opened by a man in shirtsleeves, smoking a thin cigar, whose physiognomy answered to the description given by Wiggins.

" And what do you want ?" he drawled out of the corner of his mouth in an unpleasing accent.

" Joshua Leman ?" Holmes answered him in a pleasant tone. " May we come in ?" He did not wait for an answer but pushed his way through the doorway.

" Well, if that don't beat all," exclaimed Leman. " What happened to Englishmen and their homes as their castles ?"

" You are no Englishman," retorted Holmes. " The saying has no applicability in your case."

" What are you after, anyway, and who are you ?"

" My name is Sherlock Holmes."

" I've heard of you. You make trouble for honest folk, I hear."

" I make no trouble for honest folk, but it is my business to make trouble for such as you."

" You mind your mouth, Mr. Holmes." Leman said, reaching inside his coat.

Holmes lashed out with his stick, catching Leman's wrist, and the revolver clattered to the floor.

" Naughty, naughty," Holmes admonished the American. He stopped and pocketed the pistol before swiftly withdrawing the blade from the swordstick, and pointing the tip towards Leman's throat. " You are to cease the harassment of John Harden. Lady Harden informed me the other day that she will no longer play your little game and wishes you to stop your persecution of her husband."

" I will expose him !" said Leman, with an air of quiet menace. " I hold the ace here."

" Not so. I fear that your ace will be trumped by Lady Harden and her husband, who, I am confident, will be able to explain his indiscretions to the Duke in such a way that the marriage will be preserved and your intentions thwarted. May I advise you to leave this country and return to the United States."

" I have no reason to do so."

" Oh, but indeed you do. I, along with the police here in London, have their eye on you, and you will find our judges less amenable to your methods of persuasion than yours – oh yes, I know all about the Atlanta trial, never fear. I suggest that you bear this in mind, and I bid you a good day." So saying, Holmes turned his back and walked out of the house. Leman appeared ready to spring after him, but a preventative move on my part appeared to dissuade him, and he slunk back, snarling like a wild dog deprived of its prey.

I followed Holmes out into the street, where we hailed a cab.

" It is not often that I act as a bringer of matrimonial concord," remarked Holmes, " but it appears to me that Harden is genuinely repentant, and had not acquainted his wife with the full facts of the matter concerning his remorse, out of modesty, I am sure. He strikes me as being essentially a good man, if a little weak at times."

" And Leman ?"

" I saw it in his eyes. His game is played out here in England. He will take ship across the Atlantic to the land of his birth."

Here, however, Holmes was mistaken. About two months after the events described here, we received word from Vienna that Leman had removed himself to that city, and was plying his vile trade there.

Harden and his wife appeared to be completely reconciled, if the reports in the newspapers were to be believed, and Harden himself confirmed this when he visited us. He expressed his warm appreciation of the work that Holmes had undertaken on his behalf, paying a most generous sum of money to my friend by way of a fee.

" Some of this, I believe," said Holmes, fingering the cheque, " should perhaps go to Wiggins, who has been deprived of the reward of five shillings per day for the simple task of abusing gentlemen."

" I think not," I laughed. " It is hardly a habit that should be encouraged."

And so we left the matter, though I believe that some of Harden's money did indeed eventually make its way into the pocket of that most valued leader of the Baker-street Irregulars.

THE ADVENTURE OF THE COPPER PINS

This case is mentioned in The Adventure of the Five Orange Pips. *It is less of a tale of detection than one of adventure, albeit one that showcases Holmes' skills with regard to disguise and taking on another temporary identity, as well as his knowledge of the criminal landscape of London. Another, unexpected, talent also comes to light – that of card-sharping.*

The reason why this story was not included in the original published adventures of Sherlock Holmes becomes obvious as the tale unfolds – Watson would not want this story to cast an unflattering light on the Metropolitan Police force.

Lastly, it should be mentioned that while Watson pays due tribute to Holmes' talents in regard to disguise and dissimulation, he overlooks, with characteristic modesty, his own prowess in that direction. One can hardly imagine Holmes involving Watson in an adventure with such a high degree of risk if he were not confident of Watson's being able to carry off the necessary deception.

Lichfield and Milan
April 2017

Y friend Sherlock Holmes, while not usually re-garded as the most imaginative of men in the tra-ditional sense of the word, nonetheless displayed considerable ingenuity in the different faces he displayed to the world on various occasions. His skill in disguise, not only in the matter of his dress, but also in his general demeanour, was such that he would have made his for-tune on the stage, had his fancy taken him in that particular direction.

On no occasion were these talents better displayed than in the extraordinary events I describe here, where Holmes met his near equals in the art of subterfuge and disguise, and it was only by an extraordinary application of his talents that he was able to escape with a whole skin.

The whole affair started innocuously enough with a visit from Inspector Tobias Gregson of Scotland Yard, who dropped into our rooms in Baker-street on a Thursday evening, as had become an almost regular habit of his. Sherlock Holmes regarded Gregson as one of the more promising members of the official force, and provided him with many pieces of advice, and assistance, which have, I dare say, been at least in part responsible for that officer's promotion to the high office he now holds.

" There appear to be a confoundedly large number of beggars around the West End these days," Gregson complained, puffing away at the cigar which Holmes had provided for his enjoyment.

" Indeed there are far too many," I agreed. " Why, only the other day in Piccadilly, one of the wretches caught hold of my trouser leg as I was passing, and would not let go until I threatened to call a constable. Even then, he kept following me, whining. Twopence was the sum I was forced to pay in order to rid myself of his attentions."

Sherlock Holmes smiled. " A penny was sufficient in my case, Watson," he remarked. " But I agree, they are a confounded nuisance. Can you not arrest them for vagrancy, Inspector ?" he enquired of Gregson.

" Alas, no," replied the police agent. " Each one of them can show some trade, selling matches or the like, which puts him out of our reach. We put one or two in the cells, but in each case the magistrate let them go, saying that these men were not vagrants. Every one of them had a tray of matches or trinkets that they claimed they had been offering for sale, and produced a valid licence allowing them to trade on the street. We had suspected forgery of these certificates at first, but further inspection revealed them to be all genuine. Remarkably, of the dozen or so that we examined, all had been issued within a few days of each other."

" You seem to be implying," I said to Gregson, " that these men are working together in some sort of gang."

" That is precisely my opinion," he answered me. " The sudden appearance of the large number of these men, and the fact that there are too many points in common between the way in which they ply their trade, and the circumstances surrounding the licences make it hard for me to believe it to be mere coincidence."

" I concur, Inspector," said Holmes. " It seems unlikely to me that a plague of beggars all adopting the same customs and methods should suddenly descend on the capital like this. Had there been a natural disaster or calamity in one part of the country which would propel them to London, I might understand it, but I have noticed that some of these men speak with a variety of accents : some Scots, some Irish, some North country, and some West country, in addition, that is to the native London Cockney."

" You think so ?" asked Gregson. " I had the same impression until the other day, when I was hailed by one of them, who spoke to me in what I took to be a West Country voice. My own family hails from that part of the country, and I asked him from what part of the world he originated. Though he told me that he came from Bristol, subsequent questioning revealed that he had no more knowledge of Bristol than do I of Timbuktoo or the streets of Peking."

" Indeed ? That is somewhat strange, as these gentlemen often possess a more intimate knowledge of the highways and byways of a town than do the official police. You will recall, Watson, the occasion on which George Hopton, whose 'pitch' was outside the Bank of London, was able to furnish us with the precise details of the hidden passage which the Clairvaux gang was to use in their attempted robbery of the

Bank – details of which the Governor and staff of the Bank were unaware."

" Do you, too, believe that these men are connected together in some sort of group ?" I asked Holmes.

" I do.   Have you observed, Gregson, one point in common among these men ? I do not refer to the usual beggars and vagrants who have become a part of the London landscape, but to these newcomers."

The police agent shook his head.   " I cannot say that I have, Mr. Holmes."

" I refer to the small copper-headed pin that each of these men wears in his left lapel.   It is so small a thing as to be almost unnoticeable, but as I have remarked to you previously, Gregson, it is often the most seemingly insignificant of trifles that turns out to have the greatest importance."

" I confess that I had not noticed that," confessed Gregson.

" I take it to be a badge of recognition among these men, allowing them to identify each other as members of a group or society."

" But to what end ?" I asked.   " It would seem strange to me for such men to organise themselves into a group."

" That would indeed be strange," said Holmes.   " This type of person is not usually of a kind who forms such associations.   However, consider the case of Neville St. Clair, whom we unmasked after he had plied his trade as a beggar.   You will recall that his earnings from that trade far outstripped the money that he made from his writing.   We should ask ourselves whether it would not be in the interests of a man to set up a group composed of such mendicants, on the understanding that he is to collect a certain portion of their takings."

" And what would the members of such a group receive in exchange ?" asked Gregson.

" I believe that a man who was capable of such organisation would also be capable of affording a measure of protection. For example you have mentioned that all those with whom you have so far come in contact are in possession of a licence to trade on the street, with all of these licenses being issued within days of each other. That, and the copper-headed pin that I mentioned earlier, point to the establishment of a group whose sole purpose is to extort money from honest citizens."

" You may well be correct in your assumption, Mr. Holmes," replied Gregson, shaking his head sadly, " but I do not think that there would be any legal reason to prevent such a thing, distasteful as it may be."

" If I were to... ?" Holmes began.

Gregson smiled. " I can give you no official encouragement on whatever it is you are planning." He held up a hand. " Please do not inform me of anything that you have in mind," he said to Holmes. " I wish to be able to say that I had no prior knowledge of whatever may transpire."

Holmes smiled in return. " I understand you perfectly, Inspector."

" However," Gregson continued, " I can at least ensure that your actions will not be impeded by the police. I can pass a discreet word around to make sure that you will be left alone, and if you are brought in and give your name, the case will be brought directly to my attention."

" Thank you," said Holmes.

When Gregson had left us, Holmes turned to me with a look in his eye that can best be described as " mischievous".

" It is true, Watson," he remarked, " that no crime as such is being committed, but it appears to me that there may well be more to this than meets the eye at first sight. I think it may be time for you and me to join the ranks of these men."

" I ?" I replied, somewhat horrified by the suggestion that I was to become a member of this group of common beggars, and said as much.

" Oh, I think we will discover that these are far from being common beggars. I expect to find something most interesting in our little experiment. Believe me, I do not expect us to be in any real danger. Now, are you with me ? "

" I am, " I replied, though not without some misgivings.

" Good man, " he told me. " I knew I could rely on my Watson. We must dress appropriately for the part, I think. And, " he added, seemingly as an afterthought, " I think it would be best if you were to shave off your moustache. "

" Why on earth-- ? "

" It is far too well-maintained, and kempt, if I may be permitted to coin the word, for the role you are to play. " He regarded my face, which clearly betrayed my shock and distress. " We all have our little personal vanities, Watson, but at times we must ignore them and make small temporary sacrifices. "

I confess that this speech did little, if anything, to mollify me, but I could perceive the truth of his words, and grudgingly assented to the loss of this facial feature of which, as Holmes had reminded me, I felt a strong attachment.

" What other changes do you wish me to make ? " I asked, somewhat irritated by his last request.

" We must change our general appearance, " he told me. " At present, we are far too much of the 'toff' to be acceptable candidates. We should appear to have been formerly respectable members of society, but now are somewhat down on our luck – perhaps something in the order of bank clerks who have lost their positions through some mishap of their own making. " Noting the expression of distress that I was obviously still wearing, he added, " Never fear. We have been assured that we have nothing to fear from the agents of the law. "

" I have always been willing to assist you in whatever way seems appropriate at the time, " I assured him.

" Excellent. Now let us go and assume our new identities."

It took me some time to prepare myself mentally for the change, but I selected the garments that I felt were necessary for my new role.

When I emerged from the bed-room and entered our living-room, Sherlock Holmes was there before me. He had not only put on new clothes, but seemed to have adopted a new personality. His tall frame was somewhat stooped, as if carrying some heavy burden, and his usual quick movements had been replaced by an almost slothful lassitude. His face, when he turned it to me, lacked its usual animation, and it seemed to me that I beheld a man who had recently faced many difficulties in his life. Truly, when Sherlock Holmes donned a disguise, he did not only look like the individual he was representing, but he took on the whole character of the man whose identity he assumed.

" You are still too much of the former soldier," he admonished me. " But no matter. It may be that you were cashiered and left the Army in disgrace. Yes, I think that will serve very well."

I cannot pretend that this filled me with any sense of joy or comfort, but I assented to the plan, and we left Baker-street, and headed for the City.

As Holmes had remarked, many of the beggars we encountered were wearing a small copper-headed pin in their lapels. It was so small as to be almost invisible, unless one were searching for it, but once seen, it was quite distinctive.

Holmes passed each by with a look of supreme indifference, until we came across a grizzled elderly man, one who wore one of the identifying pins.

" Good afternoon, Lionel Drew," he greeted the seeming vagrant, who gave a start.

" Who's he, when he's at home ?" answered the man, in

what seemed to my ears to be an imitation of a Northern accent.

" Why, sir," Holmes told him, " he was the man who stood trial for theft, and subsequently served a prison term for his crime."

The unkempt beggar seemed to turn pale beneath his mask of grime and dirt. " How in God's name would you know that, sir ?" he asked in frightened tones. " Are you one of the police, then ? I tell you now that I've gone straight now, sir. Reduced to begging in the streets, as you see."

" Never mind who I am," said Holmes. " I find myself in the same position as were you some years back. My friend here," indicating me, " is also in need of assistance. Maybe you can help us."

" How ?" asked the other, suspiciously.

" I believe you may be able to put us in touch with an important person." My friend reached out and touched the copper head of the pin in the other's coat lapel.

" What do you know of us ?" said Drew, obviously now terrified by my friend's knowledge of what he obviously had considered to be a secret up to that time.

" Not nearly as much as I would like," answered Holmes.

" Come back here at five," Drew said. " I'll take you. We'll see if you're accepted or not. Oh, and while you're here," he added as we started to move away, " I think that's worth at least a couple of bob."

" Very well," said Holmes, handing over the two shillings. " But if there are any false moves on your part, I will take steps to recover that money – with suitable interest, I might add."

Once away from the beggar, I could not refrain from asking Holmes how he knew the man.

" I remember his face from the days before I moved to Baker-street and met you," he told me. " When I was learning my trade, I was a habitué of the law courts, as it seemed necessary to me to acquire a knowledge of what constituted evidence in the eyes of the law. Lionel Drew was a trusted member of the management at one of London's largest hotels, but stood accused of purloining jewellery from guests' rooms over a period of several years. He was found guilty, and sentenced to a lengthy spell in prison."

" But you were not involved with the case ?"

" Officially, no. However, from the evidence that had been presented, it was obvious to me that he was guilty of the crime, though the police made a sad bungle of the accusation. Had Drew's lawyer been only slightly more astute, he would have been released. The incident was most instructive in teaching me the necessity of ensuring that one must be absolutely certain of one's evidence when presenting a case to the courts."

As we continued to stroll around the City, I could not help but notice the reaction of other pedestrians to Holmes and myself. In our unaccustomed garb and characters, the reaction of the smartly-suited gentlemen who worked in the banks and businesses of the City was one of near revulsion. It was possible to observe their distaste as we approached, and their almost imperceptible shrinking away from us, avoiding physical contact, as we came closer. On the other hand, the office-boys and messengers, who as a rule would show a certain deference, treated us with some familiarity, often jostling us, which they would never had done had we been dressed in our usual attire.

At five o'clock, we returned to the place where we had seen Drew, and it was with mixed feelings that I saw he was still in the same spot.

" So you're looking for an introduction ?" he asked Holmes, who nodded in assent. " It's only fair to warn you that if you don't join us, and you say anything about what you're going to see, then it's—" He made a gesture as if cutting a throat.

" I understand you," answered Holmes.

" Follow me, then," said Drew, picking up the greasy cap in which he had collected money from passers-by. " Somewhere between one pound ten and two pounds, I reckon," he said. " Not the best of days, but not the worst either."

I was somewhat surprised at the amount, and disturbed at the threat of violence should whatever secret was to be revealed to us be accidentally made public by either Holmes or myself. Again, my face must have shown my feelings, as Drew made some lewd and obscene comment upon it, which I will not trouble to repeat here.

We followed Drew silently through the streets of the City to the area behind the docks, through Whitechapel to Limehouse. Holmes seemed to be perfectly aware and at home in this milieu, but for myself, I continued to feel more than a little nervous.

" Well, here we are," Drew told us, stopping in front of a furniture warehouse marked with the name of a well-known firm of removers. He descended the steps at the front of the warehouse which led to what was presumably a cellar, and knocked on the door with a peculiar rhythm.

The spyhole in the door opened, and an eye appeared, which regarded us with what seemed to be a suspicious air.

" Who are these two ?" came a gruff voice.

" Applicants for the Society," said Drew.

" Do you know them ?"

" One of 'em knows me," said Drew. " God knows how, but he does. Never remember seeing him before. The other doesn't say a lot, but I reckon he's been in a spot of trouble, looking at him."

There was the sound of bolts being drawn back, and the door opened to admit us. The doorman was a near hunchback, with a villainous expression, who scowled at us as we followed Drew into the cellar.

I could not help but let out a gasp of surprise at what I saw. The spacious chamber, far from being the warehouse that I had expected, was furnished in a fashion that would not have disgraced one of the leading gentleman's clubs in the West End of the capital. Comfortable armchairs, most of which were occupied by men dressed in the most respectable of style were arranged in groups around small tables, upon which sat bottles and glasses.

Our guide chuckled as he beheld Holmes' and my surprise. " Gave you a shock, did it ?" he said, in an almost cultured voice that bore little resemblance to his previous tones. " I have to say I was more than a little taken aback when I first came here."

" Where are we ?" I asked.

" Ah, I do not believe it is really my place to tell you that. Let me take you to Atherton Spillney, who will inform you of the prerequisites for joining the Society."

I was mystified by this speech and its implications, but glancing at Holmes, it appeared that most, if not all, of this had been anticipated by him.

Drew led us to a small door at one side of the large room, and knocked. A voice bade us enter, and we found ourselves on one side of a desk, on the other of which was seated a man who was presumably Atherton Spillney.

My first impression was of grossness. His sparse sandy hair was combed back, exposing a smoothy pink forehead. His clean-shaven cheeks were a bright pink, but not the pink of a healthy nature, as a half-empty decanter and glass on the desk evinced. His many chins trembled above a thick neck, which descended into a body that appeared porcine in nature. Though at first sight he appeared to be well-dressed, closer inspection showed that his garments were not of the quality that they first appeared to be. He was smoking a large cigar, which he removed from his mouth as he regarded Holmes and me through slitted eyes.

" Who are these, Drew ?" he asked.

" He," pointing at Holmes, " knows me from a long time back – the time of my trouble, in fact.   Not sure about his friend."

" Your names ?" Spillney asked us.

Holmes spoke for us both.   " I am Patrick Kennedy, and my friend here is Martin Lafferty," he replied, with a strong Irish brogue.

" That's not the way you spoke to me earlier," complained Drew.   " He spoke almost like a toff when he met me."

" Let us assume," said Holmes, maintaining the brogue, " that my friend and I are who I say we are."

" Very well," said Spillney.   " I assume that you have run into some trouble, shall we say, recently ?" He leaned back in his chair and took a deep drag of his cigar.

Holmes, still in his role of Irishman, told a story of woe which involved the misappropriation of clients' funds from a stockbroking firm.

" And him ?" asked Spillney, jabbing a thumb in my direction.

I started to speak but Holmes anticipated me, telling a tale of how I had been cashiered from my regiment following disputes over the mess bill.

" Got any other tricks up your sleeve ?" asked Spillney.

Holmes demanded a pack of cards, which the other produced from a drawer of his desk, and proceeded to remove a queen and two jacks from the pack.

" Ha !" exclaimed Spillney.   " You had best be good at this, mister.   I used to make my living at this game."

Holmes turned all the cards face up, with the queen in the middle, then turned them face down and started to re-arrange them, following which he invited Spillney to indicate the queen.

On turning over the selected card, Holmes disclosed that it was indeed the queen.

He repeated the process, and once again Spillney selected the correct card.

" Not bad, Mr. Kennedy," he sneered. " But you've got to be better than that to beat me."

" Let us try again," said Holmes, and arranged the cards once again. This time, Spillney turned over one of the jacks, and let out an oath.

" I would have sworn that was the queen," he snarled. " One more time."

Holmes once again arranged the cards, and once more Spillney picked a jack.

" I don't know what you're doing," he said, " but it seems you're too quick for my eyes. Once more," he ordered.

The cards were spread out one more time, and Spillney gave a triumphant shout. " I saw you that time, Mr. Kennedy," he gloated, and turned over a card – which once more proved to be a jack. " Well, I was certain that time. You pulled a very handsome double-bluff just then. Once more," he ordered, but once more the jack was the chosen card. Spillney sighed. " Very good, Mr. Kennedy," he told Holmes. " I am happy to accept you as a member of the Amateur Mendicant Society. The terms are generous. You will be provided with a licence to trade on the street, and a supply of matchboxes, which you will not, of course, be required to sell. You will solicit money from the passers-by, and I suggest that you will also use the skills you have demonstrated so far to increase your earnings. You understand your duties ?"

" I do, so far," replied Holmes.

" You will also be furnished with one of these," went on Spillney, reaching in a desk drawer and extracting a copper-headed pin. " You are to wear this at all times on the street. A good number of the police force who patrol the area are aware of the significance of this pin. If they perceive you wearing it, they will leave you in peace to ply your trade."

I shuddered inwardly as I considered the implications of this. Clearly Spillney was implying that at least some members of the police force had been given instructions not to interfere with the business of these men. But who, I asked myself, would have the influence to subvert the course of justice in such a way ?

Holmes, however, appeared to take this development in his stride. " This all seems admirably arranged," he remarked. " I am assuming, though, that this is not all provided out of the goodness of a patron's heart ?"

Spillney smiled. " Of course you are correct, Mr. Kennedy. To furnish the Society's premises in the style that you observed as you entered, we operate a system whereby the members make a small weekly contribution in the nature of one third of their weekly takings. We trust our members to be honest regarding these matters, Mr. Kennedy," and here he fixed Holmes with a stare that was no doubt intended to be menacing, but which from a man of his corpulence had more of the ridiculous about it, " as you may imagine."

" And if they are not ?" Holmes enquired, with a lift of his eyebrows.

" The protection of the copper pin is removed from them, and we invoke the assistance of the police to remove them from the streets."

Once again I was inwardly appalled at the level of cooperation between this gang of rogues and the police.

" That all seems perfectly clear," said Holmes. " And my friend ?" he added, indicating me.

" He doesn't seem to have a lot to say for himself," said

Spillney. " Could he not play the 'bonnet' and take the part of a 'flat', to lure others into the game ?"

I nodded dumbly, and Holmes assented to this. " In that case, since you will be working together, I will apply the Society's usual rates in such cases, and expect one half of your takings. The Society's premises are yours to use when you are not working, as I have explained. There is food and drink available, which are yours, in moderation, and the copper pins that I am about to give you will afford you some protection from the police, as I have explained. I trust that all is explained to your satisfaction, gentlemen ?"

" Certainly," said Holmes. " One more point. You now know our history. Without going into detail, can you tell me the general history of the other members of this Society ?"

" Like yourselves, they have fallen on unfortunate times, through a variety of circumstances. Most of them do not imagine that their membership of the Society will be a permanent one, trusting that their lot will improve in the near future."

" And does this fortunate occurrence ever transpire ?"

" In a few cases, yes. In these instances, the members return their pins to me, and are bound by an oath of secrecy never to reveal anything about the Society."

" One more question, if I may ?" Spillney nodded his assent to Holmes' query. " How many members does the Society have at present ?"

Spillney opened a ledger that was lying on his desk. " You are numbers thirty-six and thirty-seven," he informed us. " When I present you with your pins, guard them, and the secrets of the Society that I have just revealed to you, with your lives."

" You do not wish us to swear an oath or some such ?" asked Holmes, smiling.

" Oh, believe me, we have much more efficient ways of

keeping our little secrets than oaths and gentlemen's words of honour and the like," said Spillney. The smile which accompanied these words was not a comfortable one. "Let me see. It is Thursday today. I shall expect to see you both at this time a week on Friday. I trust that you will have amassed a tidy sum by that time. I will leave you to arrange your own place of work, but I suggest that you maintain a suitable distance between yourselves and other members of the Society. Good evening, gentlemen."

It was clearly a dismissal, but Holmes did not move. "The pins, if you please, Mr. Spillney," he requested.

"Ah yes, how careless of me," answered the other. He held out his hand containing the pins, but it appeared to me that there was more than a little reluctance in the action. Holmes appeared to ignore this, and took the two pins, handing one to me.

"Many thanks for your assistance," said Holmes, as we took our leave.

"I look forward to seeing you next Friday," answered Spillney, but an unpleasant leer seemed to accompany his words.

We were permitted to leave by the doorman, who carefully scanned the road outside the door before opening it for us. Once outside, we started off, but in the opposite direction that from which we had arrived. I started to speak to Holmes, but I was restrained by his powerful grip on my arm.

"Not a word, Watson!" he hissed, almost inaudibly. I forbore to enquire further, but simply followed Holmes' lead as we threaded our way through a number of small streets and alleys, which were unknown to me, but seemed as familiar to Holmes as did our own Baker-street.

At length, we emerged from a thoroughfare flanked by warehouses to a small quay by the river. "We must cross to the other side," said Holmes. "That skiff there will take us."

The owner of the skiff, whoever they might be, appeared to be nowhere in sight as Holmes untied the painter and stepped into the boat. For my part, I was dubious about the morality of the exercise, but taking the view that I might as well be hanged for a sheep as for a lamb, followed him, though I first extracted a half-sovereign and laid it on the top of the post to which the boat had been tied.

" Honest to a fault, Watson," smiled Holmes as he bent to the oars. " Do you steer us for the wharf on the south bank."

I accordingly took the lines and set our course for the directed destination.

" Why are we doing this ?" I asked.

" It is important – nay, it is vital – that the man who has been following us since we left the Society does not know about Baker-street. Were he to do so, our goose would be cooked."

" You mean that we would be in danger ?"

" I believe we would be in deadly peril. This so-called 'Society' is one which speaks of an impressive organisation. There are few men who are capable of such a feat, and one of them is perhaps best described as the second most dangerous man in London. I have no wish to end up as another trophy in the bag of this famed and feared big-game hunter. Our lives would not be worth a farthing were he to be aware of our true identities."

I digested this sombre information in silence, broken only by the lapping of the water against the bows of our craft, and the distant sound of ships' sirens as they navigated the river.

" What also concerns me, as I am sure it does you and every true Englishman, is the degree to which the police force has been infiltrated and corrupted by this group of men."

" It is truly intolerable !" I burst out. " To think that the guardians of law and order can sell their allegiance in this way !"

" It has been some time since I first suspected something

of the kind," said Holmes. " Both Lestrade and Gregson have quietly voiced their suspicions to me in the past. But now we have our weapons to fight back and purge the Force of the rotten apples that have infected the barrel." He broke off. " Halloa ! Our friend seems to have found a boat of his own, but he will not be able to reach us in time." Holmes, rowing, could of course observe the scene behind us, while I was forced to turn my head in order to view the scene. " How far to the shore, Watson ?"

" A matter of fifty yards or less," I told him.

" Excellent."

It was a matter of only a few minutes before we landed, close to Greenwich, where we made straight for the nearest station of the River Police.

Upon Holmes introducing himself, the sergeant in charge was only too happy to lend his assistance to us in the shape of a ride on a police steam-launch making its way to Westminster.

Huddled below the gunwale, we hoped we were invisible to any observers, and we soon arrived at the foot of the Embankment, whence we hailed a cab to Baker-street.

" What do you propose doing ?" I asked Holmes.

" Technically, it would seem that the members of this Amateur Mendicant Society are doing nothing illegal by their begging, since they are furnished by the appropriate licences, though I have no doubt that they can be stopped from plying their trade. The true crimes to me are the suborning of the police constables and others by the leaders of the Society."

" Agreed," I said.

" I very much doubt if we will be able to apprehend Atherton Spillney and the other of which I spoke earlier. These men can vanish from the country on a whim, and we would be unable to locate, let alone apprehend, them. The immediate problem is the number of constables in the pay of this group. However, we have a pair of weapons at our disposal which we can use to pick them out and dispose of them." He held out the two copper-headed pins which we had been given. " My plan," he went on, " is that we proceed as the three-card trickster and his 'bonnet'. Your role is to play the part of a victim, and to win, thereby ensuring a steady stream of customers. Do not worry," he chuckled. " No skill will be required on your part, other than a modicum of thespian performance."

" But if you are intending to take money from the victims ? Does not your conscience bother you a little in that regard ?"

" I will ensure that they leave with as much or maybe even a little more than they started. Since the services I provided for one of the crowned heads of Europe, my bank account can stand a little strain of that nature. However, our primary task will be to note the numbers of those constables and other police officers who recognise the significance of our pins, and leave us to our devices. We can communicate these numbers to Lestrade and Gregson, who will then be in a position to purge the ranks. Once that is done, before next Friday, I think we will be able to close down the Society."

The next morning, it was with some trepidation that I donned my disguise, and set out with Holmes to start our work. We discovered a quiet corner near Moorgate, at the point where the City begins, and set to work. My part in the little comedy was simple – to play the part of a customer, and to beat Holmes' attempts to confuse me with his sleight of hand. Before long, there was a small gathering of about six men, clerks from the nearby lawyers' offices to judge from their appearance, with one of them clamouring for a chance to win money.

Holmes played him skilfully, like an angler with a trout, allowing him to win, to lose, to win again, so that by the time the clerk had tired of the game, he walked away, as Holmes had promised, with the same amount of money as when he started.

Another stepped into his place, and Holmes was about to deal the cards when we were interrupted by a police constable, whose considerable bulk blocked the light.

" I'd like a word with you," he addressed Holmes, to a chorus of disapproval from the group of clerks.

Holmes stood up and faced the policeman, making sure that the copper pin in his lapel was clearly visible. I could see the constable's surprise as he registered the sight, and his expression changed. " Make sure you do not block the pavement," he admonished Holmes, and walked off without another word. I had meanwhile made a note of his number.

The process was repeated twice more during the day, with two different constables also noticing the copper pins in our lapels, and walking away with a cursory warning.

That evening, we made our way back to Baker-street by a circuitous route, Holmes having assured himself that we were not being followed. After we had changed our attire, Holmes sent a message to Gregson, who visited us shortly.

" A fine piece of work, Mr. Holmes," he said, on hearing our report, and receiving the numbers of the three constables whom we suspected of being in league with the Amateur Mendicants Society. " Do you wish to continue your operations in another part of town ? Piccadilly, or Marble Arch, for example ?"

" I would prefer to concentrate my efforts around the City," Holmes told him. " I believe that we will attract more crowds of the type we attracted today – the younger clerks out to prove the sharpness of their natures to each other. The important thing is that we finish our work before Friday, so that you may close down this Society by arresting Spillney, though I very much doubt whether you will be able to touch the man behind this operation."

" We will move on Thursday night," Gregson assured him, " and not before. In the meantime, we would be grateful if you and the Doctor here could identify as many of the rotten apples in the Force as possible before that time. We will strike at them at the same time that we strike at the head."

On receiving Holmes' word that this would be the case, the police agent left us.

The next few days were a repetition of the first. Naturally, the same constables (and not a few sergeants) became familiar to us, but by the allotted time, Holmes and I had amassed a list of over a dozen numbers of those policemen who had reacted to the sight of our copper pins.

" I do not wish to accompany you on this expedition," Holmes informed Gregson and Lestrade, both of whom were visiting our rooms at Baker-street early on the Thursday evening. Were I to be recognised, either as Patrick Kennedy or as Sherlock Holmes, it would upset my plans for bringing to justice the men behind all this. The time is not yet ready, but when it is, rest assured that I will strike, and strike hard."

" Very well, Mr. Holmes," said Lestrade. " The part of Gregson here in this is to remove the rogue elements from the Metropolitan Police, while I will be leading the charge against the Society's premises. Between you and me, Mr. Holmes, we have had our eye for some time on a number of the constables that you identified, but others were completely unsuspected."

The raid was a complete success. The Society was broken up, and Atherton Spillney was brought to trial, on the charge of selling intoxicating liquor without a licence to do so, there being little else with which he could be charged. The dismissal and subsequent prosecution of the offending constables, which in turn led to several more being dismissed from the Force, was widely applauded in official circles, and both

Holmes and I received personal letters of thanks from the Home Secretary.

" I feel, Watson," Holmes remarked to me at the conclusion of all these events," that as interesting a diversion as this has proved to be, it would not be in the interests of the nation to divulge the details of this case.   Though," he added, with a twinkle, " your readers might be tantalised by the mention of the Amateur Mendicant Society, provided, of course, that you added no details.   And it also strikes me that should the business of detection suffer a decline, it would be possible for you and me to earn our living at three-card monte."

THE ADVENTURE OF THE DECEASED DOCTOR

T was Christmas of 1916 – that terrible winter following the fighting on the Somme, where so many of our gallant young men lost their lives in the mud of Northern France, and so many had been killed on the Turkish shores of the Dardanelles. For my part, I had re-joined the colours, but my duties were in " Blighty", as we had learned to call our native land, where I worked in a Hampshire hospital treating those who were recovering from the loss of a limb or severe head wounds.

Since providing assistance to my old friend Sherlock Holmes in the matter of the arrest of the German spy, Von Bork, he and I had maintained a correspondence, and from him I learned of his elder brother Mycroft's death some years previously as the result of an aneurism. Sherlock Holmes himself was employed in matters which had previously formed part of his brother's remit, and from the guarded hints that he dropped in his letters to me, he was dividing his time between his bees in Sussex and the Admiralty, where he had dealings with a mysterious organisation in that building which went by the name of " Room 40". Naturally, as a patriotic citizen, I did not enquire further into the nature of his work, and he, by his very nature, was secretive regarding it.

It was, as I say, Christmas-time, and I had invited Holmes to spend the holiday season with me. My fellow-lodger had recently departed for the Front, and I considered it to be a kindness to Mrs. Dalwymple (the landlady of my " digs", whom I discovered after having lodged there for some months to be a distant cousin of dear Mrs. Hudson of Baker-street) to invite Holmes to take the room for a week or so at my expense, as well as providing me (and, I hoped, Holmes) with congenial company.

Much to my delight, he had accepted my invitation, and he arrived, showing signs of age, which I fear were not only due to the passing of the years, but also to the terrible strain and stress that he was suffering as a result of his Admiralty work. He was, as was his nature, reticent about the details, but from my knowledge of Holmes, I could read between the lines that a terrible responsibility lay upon his shoulders as the result of his duties.

" I am delighted to see you, Watson," he greeted me as he entered the house. " And back in harness. You appear to be in good health, though you have lost a little weight. Five and one-quarter pounds, I fancy, since I saw you last."

I laughed. " Holmes, I do not have time or the inclination to worry about such things. I dare say you, as always, are correct. Ah, Mrs. Dalwymple," I added as my landlady approached, " may I introduce my old friend, Mr. Holmes."

" Pleased to meet you, sir," she said to him. " Doctor Watson has told me that you used to lodge in London with my cousin, Mrs. Martha Hudson."

" Indeed so. Happy days, were they not, eh, Watson ? I hope you will not take it amiss, Mrs. Dalwymple, if I make you a present of these." He held out two jars of honey. " They are from my own hives on the South Downs, and I will wager that it is some of the finest honey you will ever taste."

" Oh, Mr. Holmes !" she exclaimed. " With the rationing and everything as it is now, this is most welcome. You keep bees, then, sir ?"

" Indeed I do. Forty hives, forty little kingdoms, or should I say ' queendoms', each busy in the pursuit of sweetness."

" Why, Holmes, you are quite poetic," I laughed.

" Apiculture is a subject fit for poetry. You remember your Virgil, Watson ? The Georgics, Book Four ?"

" A cup of tea, Mr. Holmes ?" Mrs. Dalwymple offered.

" It would be most welcome," he answered, and I ushered him into the drawing-room that was used by the lodgers of the house as a common-room. Currently, I was the only lodger, and was therefore able to treat the room as my own.

After ascertaining that my landlady had no objection to tobacco, Holmes filled and lit his pipe, and leaned back in his armchair. " Ah, Watson," he sighed, " you have no idea what pleasure it gives me to see that familiar face seated opposite me. The memories of those days..."

" You are becoming sentimental in your old age, Holmes."

" Am I ? I suppose it is a state that we all approach as time passes. But it is true, is it not, that those days which you recorded so sensationally were indeed some of the best of our lives ?"

He and I fell into reminiscences, interrupted only by the arrival of the tea-tray, graced with a steaming teapot, and with some scones adorned with some of Holmes' own honey. I learned that Lestrade had recently retired, with the rank of Superintendent, and that Tobias Gregson, one of the Force's more promising officers, according to Holmes, had recently been rewarded with a knighthood.

" And you yourself, Holmes ? Why are you not now Sir Sherlock Holmes ? The nation owes you that, and much more, for your services over the years."

" The honour has been offered to me on a number of occasions," he said. " What need have I for such a bauble ? My fame, such as it is, is the result of your work, and requires no further adornment. As for those who rule us, believe me when I say that they are well enough aware of my little contributions to the security of our realm." He paused, and yawned. " As am I. The work on which I am currently engaged is devilish tiring at times."

" Would you permit me to examine you at some time while you are here ?" I asked him. " I am certain that it is some time since you have visited a medical practitioner."

" If it will amuse you," he answered. " You are correct in your supposition, though. I seem to have had little time for such matters recently."

I had detected, during our conversation, various signs of fatigue and strain, similar to those I had observed in our shell-shocked patients. The twitching eyelid and slight trembling motion of the hand were symptoms I had also observed before in Holmes when he had driven his body and spirit to their limits. There was an additional air of " nerves" about Holmes which was remarkably pronounced, even for him.

The evening passed pleasantly enough, however, in friendly conversation, punctuated at times by those silences which can be said to be companionable, and whose existence is only possible with those between whom a deep friendship exists.

" I am for bed," I told Holmes as the clock struck ten. " I must make the rounds of the wards early tomorrow morning, although it is Christmas Eve. I expect to be finished and to have returned by half-past eight, and we may breakfast together on my return, if that is agreeable to you."

" Perfectly agreeable," he answered.

 T was five o'clock in the morning as I made my way through the darkened wet streets to the hospital. As I approached, I was surprised to see more lights in the windows than I would expect to see at that hour.

I entered the building and was instantly accosted by the nursing sister who was in charge overnight.

" Doctor Watson !" she exclaimed breathlessly. " Thank goodness you are here. Come with me now !"

" Why, what is the matter ?" I asked her. " Surely there is nothing that Doctor Godney cannot manage ?" I should add that our patients were for the most part convalescent, and did not require the kind of intensive medical attention that was needed at the Front, for example.

" Doctor Godney," she answered me with a sniff, " is

dead. He is sitting there in his office, at his desk, but cold as ice."

I was naturally shocked at this news and expressed my surprise that such a seemingly healthy young man should pass away so suddenly.

" But that is not the worst," she added. " Come and see for yourself."

She led the way to the room, where, as I had been told, Godney was sitting at his desk, motionless. On the floor was visible, protruding from behind the desk, a pair of legs, shod, but otherwise bare to the knee, and female, if the shoes on the feet were any guide.

" Who is that ?" I asked, pointing to the legs.

" Nurse de Lacey. One of our volunteers."

I remembered the girl, who was working at the hospital to " do her bit". She was an exceedingly pretty young lady, from one of our old county families, and seemed always willing to help with even the most menial of tasks, which would have turned the stomach of many lesser women.

" She is also dead ?" I asked, horrified by this revelation.

" No. Merely unconscious."

" And you have left her there ? Why ?"

" See for yourself, Doctor," was the reply.

By now it was clear to me that foul play of some kind had been done. I therefore stepped with extreme caution around the side of the room, taking care to cause as little disturbance as possible, and beheld the scene from the far side of the desk.

" You are sure he is dead ? What have you moved or touched ?" I asked.

" I am sure, Doctor," she answered me. " I have touched as little as possible. Both of them are in the same place and posture as when I discovered them. I did only what was necessary to confirm the presence or absence of life."

" It was you who discovered this scene, then ?"

" It was I. One of my patients was coughing, and I came to the office to obtain the key to the dispensary from Doctor Godney. I knocked, and there was no answer, so I let myself in, and saw— this."

" When did you discover this ?"

" Not ten minutes before you arrived, Doctor."

" And who else knows of these events ?"

" No-one other than you. If you had not arrived when you did, I was about to alert Perkins, the porter, and ask him to inform the police."

" Very well," I told her. I surveyed the scene. Sister Lightfoot was experienced enough for me to be able to take her word regarding the condition of the two bodies. It was clear, in any case, that Nurse de Lacey was alive, but appeared at first sight to be in no danger. However, the garments comprising the upper half of her nurse's outfit, as well as the undergarments beneath, were opened at the front, almost to the waist, and nearly exposing her breasts, which rose and fell gently in time with her shallow breathing. Her skirts had been pulled up to a little above the knee, and it was clear that her stockings had been pulled down. Her body appeared to be lying on a hypodermic syringe, half of which was visible.

" The hussy," said the sister, as she took in my shock at seeing the partly-undressed body lying there.

" It is not for us to judge others, Sister," I told her sharply. " Now listen to me and follow my orders. You are to tell Perkins and ask him to fetch the police, as you were about to do. Having done that, you are to return immediately with a blanket, and use it to cover Nurse de Lacey. You are then to stand outside the door and permit no-one to enter, including the police. We are lucky in that my old friend Sherlock Holmes is presently staying with me. I am sure that he will be able to provide answers to the questions that we all have regarding the death of Doctor Godney, and the unfortunate condition of Nurse de Lacey." I spoke in a tone of voice befitting the nominal Army rank of Captain which had been bestowed on me on my appointment to the hospital. " While you inform Perkins, I will stand guard here until your return with the blanket, and then fetch Mr. Holmes."

" Yes, Doctor," she replied meekly. When she had gone, I moved as carefully as I could to Godney, and satisfied myself that life was indeed extinct. Sister Lightfoot's first words, that he was cold, were mistaken. Given the temperature of the room, which was well heated, I estimated that he had passed away not more than a few hours previously, but it was impossible for me to be sure of that without more precise measurements. However, it was clear that rigor had yet to set in, and this likewise confirmed my suspicions.

I had completed my preliminary investigations when Sister returned, bearing a blanket, which I helped her spread over Miss de Lacey.

" Very good, Sister," I told her, instructing her to wait outside until I returned with Sherlock Holmes. " I will be as quick as possible," I told her.

Much to my relief, Sherlock Holmes was awake and dressed when I reached Mrs. Dalwymple's, though it was barely six o'clock.

" Back so soon ?" he asked me.

" I am glad to see you awake," I answered.

" I found it hard to sleep, and accordingly arose early. Surely breakfast is not prepared at this hour ?"

" By no means. You are needed at the hospital urgently. There has been a death, and I suspect murder."

His face brightened. " How very gratifying. I mean to say that it is gratifying you feel that I may still be of use in these matters," he added hurriedly. " A murder, you say ? Well, well. Just like old times, indeed."

He dressed for the chill outdoors, and as we hurried through the streets, I informed him of the circumstances.

" Dear me," he exclaimed, as I informed him of the partially undressed state of Miss de Lacey. " I fear we will be uncovering matters which the principals in the case would best have left hidden."

We arrived at the hospital, to discover Sister Lightfoot standing outside the door, with an elderly uniformed constable beside her.

" I've heard of your work in the past, Mr. Holmes," the policeman informed him, " and I'm no detective myself, being the only man free when the porter came to the station, so I took this lady's word that I wasn't to enter until you came here. I can't speak for Inspector Braithwaite, though, who is our senior detective officer. He's been called, and should be with us shortly."

Holmes introduced himself to the sister, and thanked her gravely for her promptitude and professional conduct in the matter, words which seemed to please her. When he chose to be, Sherlock Holmes could be the most pleasing and emollient of personalities, and it was good for me to see that this faculty had not deserted him.

Without entering the room, he opened the door, and peered inside. " I trust that your Inspector Braithwaite will not be too long in arriving," he said to the constable. " It is important that we examine the scene of the crime as soon as possible after the event, but I do not propose to make an examination without the permission of the police. I have no wish to interfere where my presence is unwelcome."

" Speaking for myself, sir, I am more than happy to see you here. Many of our best men have gone over to France, sir, and Inspector Braithwaite, though he is— Ah, here he is now, sir," he broke off, drawing himself up to attention as a tall figure, accompanied by Perkins, was visible at the end of the corridor, and made its way towards us.

" Thank you, Constable. You may stand easy," said the newcomer, with more than a hint of a Northern accent to his voice. He turned to Sherlock Holmes. " You are Doctor Watson ?"

Holmes smiled and shook his head. " No, sir. This man," indicating me, " is Doctor Watson. My name is Sherlock Holmes."

" Indeed ? Bless my soul ! I had imagined you to be retired from the business of detection. This is indeed an honour, Mr. Holmes. May I ask what you are doing here ?"

" I am spending the season with my friend, Doctor Watson."

" I see. And you," addressing me, " discovered the body ?"

" It was Sister Lightfoot here who made the discovery, and brought it to my attention when I arrived for the early ward rounds this morning."

" Very good." He proceeded to question the sister, who repeated what she had told me earlier.

" Thank you. Excellent," he said to her. " Constable, go with Sister here to another room, and take her statement, and then return to the station. Now," turning to me, " you have been in the room and seen the body ?"

" I have," I told him, and informed him of my actions to date.

" We will require your statement later, Doctor. And you, Mr. Holmes ?"

" I was waiting for your arrival before I entered the room. I judged it best that it be left undisturbed as far as possible."

" Thank you for your consideration, but to tell you the truth, Mr. Holmes, I am a relative novice at this kind of work. With the war, and so many of our officers leaving to fight the Hun, we all find ourselves in unfamiliar employment, do we not ? I am content to let you work the magic of which we have all read in the accounts by Doctor Watson here, and to watch and, with luck, to learn from you."

" Very well, then," said Holmes. " I will endeavour to live up to my reputation."

It was a joy to me to see my friend in his element once more. His eyes fairly glittered as he entered the room and took in the scene. He sniffed the air.

" Do you not smell it ?" he asked me.

" What is it ?" I answered. At the time I was suffering from a mild cold, and my sense of smell was dulled.

" There is a faint scent of rose water."

" No doubt it is the scent worn by the nurse, de Lacey, is it not ?" commented Braithwaite.

" Almost certainly that is not the case," I corrected him. " The nurses at this hospital are under strict instructions not to wear any kind of jewellery or to use cosmetics or scent of any kind while on duty. The matron here strictly enforces these matters."

" The doctor, then ?" suggested the policeman.

" I have never known him to wear such," I said.

By this time, Holmes had reached the bodies, and swiftly ascertained that life was extinct in that of Godney. " How long do you estimate he has been dead, Watson ?" he asked me.

" Judging from a very rough estimation of the temperature of the body and of the rigor that I made earlier, I would say a few hours at the very most."

" I concur," said Holmes. " What would you take to be the cause of death ?"

" I have no certain idea," I replied, " but I will undertake that the syringe here that you observe has some connection."

" At what time would he commence his duties ?"

" At eight last evening, and he would make two ward rounds

in the course of the night until he ceased to be on duty at six in the morning."

" Very well," answered Holmes, and bent to the fallen nurse, removing the blanket with which she had been covered. " Ha !" he exclaimed, following a brief examination of the clothing that now only partially covered the poor girl's body. " Did you examine her ?"

" I only ensured that she was alive and not in immediate danger," I answered, with a slight blush.

" Then you did not observe that these garments appear to have been torn open by sheer force ? See, here, where two buttons are missing. I am sure your dragon of a matron would never allow a nurse to appear with a missing button."

" Indeed so."

Holmes gently opened one of the girl's eyelids. " You observe the contracted pupil ?" he asked me.

" One of the symptoms of opioid poisoning ?"

" Indeed."

The inspector had been watching Holmes at work in an embarrassed silence. He now broke in with, " Is it not time that you covered the poor lass and sent her to her bed ?"

" One minute, please. Watson, you are a medical man. One last thing. Please ensure that Miss de Lacey's nether undergarments are in place."

" What in the name of— ?" began Braithwaite, but then stopped as the implication of Holmes' request struck him. I was deeply embarrassed at having to perform this task, but a quick inspection was enough to reassure me.

" All appear to be in place and untouched," I was able to report, with a certain sense of relief.

" Very good," said Holmes. " Watson, you are familiar with the workings of this place. I will restore Miss de Lacey to some sort of state of modesty, while you summon aid to transport her to somewhere where she can be cared for."

When I returned, with two porters bearing a stretcher, and accompanied by Sister Lightfoot, who had completed her statement to the constable, the stricken nurse was now in a decent state.

" I suppose we are to move this Jezebel to a bed ?" snapped the sister.

" I fear you misjudge her," Holmes said gently. " Her upper garments seem to have been torn from her by main force. It does not appear at all possible that she removed them herself. And Doctor Watson here assures me that all is as it should be below the waist, as it were."

" Based on my cursory examination, that is," I added.

" So the poor girl was the victim of an assault by Doctor Godney ?" Sister Lightfoot's attitude appeared to change dramatically on hearing Holmes' words.

" She appears to be the victim of an assault, certainly," Holmes answered her. " As to who was the perpetrator, I agree that Doctor Godney would appear to be guilty, but, as I remarked once to Watson, and he has never let the world forget these words, it is a capital mistake to theorise before one has data."

The porters carefully lifted the unconscious girl onto the stretcher, and carried her away, the sister following. Holmes carefully picked up the syringe on which she had been lying, and placed it on one side of the desk.

" So, Inspector," said Holmes, rubbing his hands together, " what do you make of it so far ?"

" I would call it an open and shut case," said Braithwaite. " The girl came to the office, he assaulted her, she resisted his advances, and in self-defence she used this syringe here to protect her honour. In the struggle, she also received a dose of the drug with which she poisoned him."

" Good, Inspector. A fair summary of the facts as you

perceive them, but not, unfortunately, of the facts that are to hand.

" Consider the following. We are told that under no circumstances are the nurses or staff permitted to wear scent or toilet water or perfume, and yet, when we entered this room there was a distinct smell of rose water. I think we are all satisfied that this did not emanate from Doctor Godney, nor Miss de Lacey.

" Next, we have the evidence of the ripped clothing," he continued. " Two buttons were torn off the bodice. Where are those buttons ?"

" Maybe they are still with Miss de Lacey, hidden in folds of her clothing ?" I suggested.

" It is certainly possible," answered Holmes, " and you may be sure that if they were, I would not be the one to find them. Watson, I intensely dislike using you as my Mercury, but you are a member of the staff here, and you have the authority to command. Can you please ask the sister to search Miss de Lacey's clothing for the missing buttons or any scraps of torn cloth, or threads ? Thank you."

I left on my errand, and returned to discover Holmes examining the hypodermic syringe with his lens. " Well now, what do you make of that ?" he asked me, passing me the lens.

" The plunger is halfway down the barrel, and I see some traces of blood on the needle, but yet I see no sign of any liquid having been recently contained in there," I said, a little perplexed.

" Indeed so. And now look at this." With a forefinger he lifted one eyelid of the corpse, to display an eye that appeared perfectly normal. " You recall de Lacey's eye ?"

" Indeed I do. We agreed that it showed the symptoms typical of poisoning by an opiate, did we not ?"

" We did. And if the doctor here perished by the same means, we would expect to find the same symptoms here. We do not find them, therefore we may conclude that Godney met his end by some other means."

" But the syringe," exclaimed Braithwaite. " What is the significance of that if, as you say, it did not contain a fatal drug ?"

Holmes said nothing, as he searched through the papers contained in the wastepaper basket beside the desk. " Aha !" he said, with an air of triumph, holding up two small crumpled scraps of dark brown paper. " I had guessed there would be something of the sort here."

" What are they ?" asked the policeman, as Holmes laid them on the desk beside the syringe.

" Smell them," Holmes invited, by way of answer.

Obediently, Braithwaite did so. " Chocolate !" he cried triumphantly. " With a strange bitter aroma added."

" There," said Holmes, " you have the method by which the drug was administered to de Lacey."

He bent to the desk, where Godney's curled hands still rested, and after first requesting and receiving permission from Braithwaite to examine the body, opened the right hand. Clutched within it were two buttons, which matched those I had observed on de Lacey's bodice. Without removing them from the dead man's palm, he applied his lens to them and examined them closely. Abruptly he stood up, with a sudden intake of breath and handed the lens first to Braithwaite, and then to me, inviting us to examine the objects.

Tell me," he said to me suddenly, " was Godney married ?"

" He was, I believe. I did not know him well, but I recall his discussing marriage at some times in the past."

" And was he in favour of the blessed state ?"

" By no means," I laughed. " He regarded a wife as a drag on a man's ambitions, and even an ambitious wife as being a handicap to success. He was by no means averse to female company, however." I broke off. " This is merely hearsay, and my word regarding a colleague. I hope you will not regard it as merely idle chatter."

" Let me be the judge of that. I know you too well of old, Watson, for me to dismiss your words lightly."

" At any rate, the story was that the nurses, particularly the younger and prettier ones, refused to be alone in a room with him. There were tales of unwanted words and worse. I repeat, though, that this is merely such gossip as tends to circulate within a small community such as this hospital."

" Nonetheless," retorted Holmes, " it may well prove to be of considerable importance. In your opinion, is it possible that Godney might have attempted to force his attention on Miss de Lacey, after summoning her to his office on some pretext ?"

" I must reluctantly admit that such an action would indeed be possible."

" And what, do you think, would Miss de Lacey's reaction be ?"

" Without doubt, she would repulse his advances."

" You seem very sure of your answer, Watson."

" I am indeed. There is a precedent."

" Oh ?" Holmes arched his eyebrows.

" This is merely gossip once more, you understand, but I have every reason to believe it true. The story is that Godney attempted to steal a kiss from Miss de Lacey about a week ago. She not only refused to accept his attention, but delivered a ringing slap to his face. This latter action was reportedly witnessed by two other nurses who happened to be passing, and the news of the incident was all around the hospital inside an hour. Since that time, Godney had been avoiding any intercourse with others in the hospital, save when his duties demanded his presence."

" Embarrassed, was he, eh ?" asked Braithwaite. I nodded.

" Given his misogyny, which is typical, may I add, of many

such womanisers, it would seem likely that he would seek his revenge on the woman who had shamed him, as he would see it," said Holmes. He broke off abruptly as there was a knock on the door.

Sister Lightfoot entered in answer to Holmes' invitation. " There were no loose buttons or threads in her clothing, though there were some missing from her bodice."

" Thank you, Sister," answered Holmes. " Then we have them here," and he showed the buttons clutched in the dead man's hand.

She shrank back at the sight of them. " Then he got what he deserved," she said. " I am sorry for the names I called that poor girl just now, but I sincerely believed that she had fallen a victim to his evil ways. Doctor Godney was a danger to any woman near him, Mr. Holmes. I do not flatter myself that I am still young or beautiful, but even I was not immune to his unwelcome attentions. As for the younger nurses," she shrugged, " they refused to be alone with him. Though I complained about him to the Superintendent, nothing was done and he persisted in his ways. Doctors are scarce in this time of war, and good doctors even more so, and Doctor Godney, for all his personal faults, was a good doctor."

" You say that the nurses feared to be alone with him ? So when you discovered the two together, you feared the worst ?"

" Indeed I did. I do not know if Doctor Watson has informed you of last week's incident ?"

" He has."

" My immediate thought was that Godney had invited her to his office early in the morning, while they were both on night duty, on the pretence of making some sort of amends for his earlier behaviour, and she had succumbed to his advances. But the fact that you have found these buttons clasped in his hand would seem to indicate otherwise."

" Indeed so," replied Holmes. " One more question, if I

may, Sister," he added as she turned to go. " Watson has informed me that the nurses and other staff here are forbidden the use of scent or toilet water."

She nodded. " That is so."

" So you would have no idea from where the scent of rose water might originate ?"

" What a question, Mr. Holmes. It is, as you know, a popular fragrance."

" Of course. But please cast your mind back to when you might last have encountered it."

She appeared lost in thought for a minute, and then came to with a start. " Yes, I do remember," she told us. " It was about three weeks ago. Captain Cardew's widow."

" Pray continue." Holmes by now was occupying one of the chairs in the office, his eyes half-closed and his fingers steepled in that attitude I knew so well.

" Captain Cardew was one of our patients. The poor man had been severely wounded by a grenade, and had lost both legs below the knee, and his entire right arm. He was suffering from shell-shock, and his constitution was extremely weak. You will vouch for that, Doctor Watson."

" Indeed. He was not under my particular care, but I attended him on a number of occasions, and it was a source of wonder to me that he hung onto life as he did."

" In any event, he died some three weeks ago, and his widow came here to view him before the undertakers arrived. I distinctly remember the smell of rose water at that time."

" Had she been a frequent visitor to the hospital before her husband's death ?"

" Why, yes. She came to see him, even if it was only for a few minutes, almost every day."

" And the doctor responsible for his care was Doctor Godney ?"

" Yes, he was. How did you guess ?"

" No guessing was involved, Sister. Thank you." It was a clear dismissal, and Sister Lightfoot took herself off.

Following Holmes' orders, I arranged for Godney's body to be removed from the office and taken to the morgue.

" I am baffled," said Braithwaite when the stretcher had left the room. " I see nothing but confusion."

" On the contrary, my dear Braithwaite, the case is now as clear as daylight. And speaking of which, the sun is at last risen, and Watson and I are ready for our breakfast. Come, let us return to the estimable Mrs. Dalwymple's. Will the addition of another guest for breakfast inconvenience her in any way, do you think ?"

" It is hard to tell in these days of rationing," I said, " but I am sure that she will manage."

" Thank you," said Braithwaite, " but I fear you are playing some sort of joke on me. I completely fail to see what you have deduced from this ?"

" Never mind," Holmes told him. " All will become clear soon."

Following breakfast, which Mrs. Dalwymple provided for the three of us with seemingly little trouble, we made our way, at Holmes' request, to the police station.

" Do you know this Mrs. Cardew, Inspector ?" Holmes asked.

" I hardly know her, Mr. Holmes. We move in somewhat different social circles, you understand. Of course I know who she is, and something about her. Her family owns the big house in one of the villages hereabouts."

" Send one of your constables to bring her to the station."

" To arrest her ?" Braithwaite appeared horrified.

" That is for you to decide when you have heard her answers to the questions which I, with your permission, propose to put to her."

" Very well, Mr. Holmes, but I fear for my position, such as it is, should you be mistaken in this matter."

" Never fear, Inspector," Holmes answered gaily, clapping the man on the shoulder.

It was some thirty minutes later that Mrs. Geraldine Cardew was shown into the room in the police station where we sat waiting. She was a striking young woman, and her widow's weeds did little to obscure the obvious beauty of her face and figure. Her expression, however, was one of stiff arrogance.

As she sat down, I noted the smell of rose water, with which she had clearly scented herself.

" Well, Sergeant," she addressed Braithwaite, " I hope you have a good reason for bringing me here. You could have visited me at the Hall and saved a poor widow the trouble of this visit."

" It is not Inspector Braithwaite, but I who requested your presence," Holmes informed her. " Thank you for your cooperation." He made a small half-bow in her direction.

" And you, sir, are.. ?"

" The name is Sherlock Holmes." There was a sharp intake of breath. " The name is familiar to you, I see."

" You are the private detective, then ? I am flattered that you lower yourself to speak to me." The tone was half-amused, and mixed with sarcasm.

" Firstly, I wish to inform you that Doctor Godney at the hospital passed away last night."

" Why should I be concerned about the death of a doctor there ?"

" He treated your husband, did he not ?"

She frowned as if in an attempt to remember, but to my eyes unconvincingly. " Yes, I recall him."

" And he also comforted you in the time of your husband's illness, did he not ?"

" He was sympathetic, yes."

" And he made himself agreeable to you ?"

" If you say so, Mr. Holmes."

" Agreeable enough for you to have your photograph taken together ?" Holmes reached in his pocket and produced a pasteboard square which he tossed onto the table.

She blanched at the sight of the photograph which showed her and the late Godney together. " Very well, then. Yes, I loved him, and I believed he loved me." She paused. " Do I have to continue ?" Holmes said nothing, but nodded silently. " My poor Giles – my husband – was a broken man. Even if his body ever healed, he would be forever only part of a man. I needed a man, Mr. Holmes, a man to hold me and care for me. Perhaps you have never felt the need of another, but for me it was a necessity, even as I watched Giles slip away from this life. Lionel Godney was that other. He appeared to me to be good and kind, and attentive."

She paused, and dabbed at her eyes with a handkerchief. " Please continue," Holmes invited. " It will go easier on you at the trial."

She started at these words, but resumed her narrative. " Then I discovered from a friend, in the week after Giles had died, that I was not the only one in his life. In fact, he had an unsavoury reputation as regards women. There were tales of his advances on the nurses at the hospital. I heard that he had been forcing his attention on Olivia de Lacey, and that was the last straw as far as I was concerned."

" She is known to you ?"

" Her family's lands run next to those of my family. We have known each other since childhood, though I confess I am a little older than her. At any rate, I was not prepared to lose Lionel to her."

" She rebuffed him, you know," I told her.

" I did not know that last night." She took a deep

breath. " You want to know how it all happened, Mr. Holmes. I will tell you, then. I knew that Lionel had the night duty last night, and I knew that he spent most of the time in his office. Earlier in the day I had come to the hospital, and hid myself in one of the unused rooms along the same corridor as his office, from which I could observe the comings and goings. At about four o'clock or a little after, according to my watch, I observed Olivia de Lacey enter his office, and I was filled with a jealous rage.

" I crept along the corridor, and flung open the door, hoping to catch the couple in what I believe you detectives call in *flagrante delicto*. Instead, I found Olivia sprawled on the floor, seemingly lifeless, and Lionel standing over her, a look of horror on his face.

" I forced him to sit down in his chair—"

" Excuse me," broke in Holmes, " but how did you manage that ?"

" I had Giles' service revolver in my hand," she replied simply. " It was unloaded, but Lionel Godney did not know that, so it was easy to force him to do my bidding. When I demanded an account of what was happening, he explained that he had lured Olivia to his office on the pretext of apologising for some previous incident, but had intended rather to take advantage of her. To that end, he had prepared some sweetmeats – chocolates – laced with laudanum, but it seemed that he had miscalculated the dose, and she had fallen to the floor, lifeless, almost immediately after eating two of them."

" Her fatigue may also have accelerated the effect," I added. " The nurses are being asked to perform work over and above the call of duty."

" Be that as it may, Olivia was lying on the floor, dead, and Lionel, the coward, was shaking in his shoes. I was so angry that I forgot the revolver was not loaded, and pulled the trigger. He burst into laughter which was almost hysterical, and that inflamed me still further. I pushed the revolver back into my skirt pocket, and snatched up the first thing I could find to hurt him."

" The hypodermic syringe that he had used to inject the laudanum into the chocolates and had subsequently cleaned, and left to dry on his desk before returning it to its proper place ?"

" Yes, I suppose so. At any rate, it was sharp, and it was in my hand, and it went in under his arm. There was remarkably little blood, I remember, but in a matter of minutes, he clutched at his chest, and appeared to lose consciousness. It soon became obvious to me that he was dead. I was glad, Mr. Holmes, glad, I tell you.

" My next move was to blacken his name without, I hoped, blackening that of Olivia de Lacey, whom, it seemed, I had misjudged. It hurt me in my heart to do this, but in my frenzy it seemed to me to be the best for all. I opened Olivia's garments roughly, exposing her flesh, not caring if I tore the cloth. I had noticed that for some reason her stockings were down about her knees. I assumed that this was as a result of her suspender belt having ' gone'." Here she made a wry grimace. " I do not expect you gentlemen to fully understand the mysteries and complexities of these things. You must take it from me that this is sometimes the case. In any event, I wished to emphasise that her upper legs were bare, and I pulled her skirts up so that the fact was obvious to all. I hoped that the implication was that Godney had assaulted her, and she had stabbed him with the syringe, which I tucked under her body."

" Did you not realise that she was still alive ?" asked Holmes.

To my amazement, Mrs. Cardew burst into peals of laughter. " She was alive ?"

" She lives," I confirmed, " and will recover soon, it is to be hoped."

" So all my ingenuity was in vain, it would seem ? Poor Olivia. But I wished that Lionel would suffer in death, so I removed some buttons from her bodice and placed them in his dead hand, and curled the fingers over them."

" The intention being to make it appear as if he had ripped open her garments, tearing off buttons in his haste ?"

" Precisely."

" You should have torn off the buttons, not snipped them off with scissors," Holmes told her. " Better yet to have left them as they were."

" How do you know that I used scissors ?" Mrs. Cardew fairly gasped.

" Elementary. A high-powered lens uncovers many secrets."

Braithwaite, who had remained silent throughout this whole conversation, now spoke. " Geraldine Cardew, I arrest you for the wilful murder of Lionel Godney on the morning of December 24, 1916. I warn you that anything you say will be taken down and used as evidence against you. Take her to the cells," he instructed a constable. " I will take her formal statement later."

Before she was led away, Mrs. Cardew requested and was granted permission to address Sherlock Holmes. Her words were as follows.

" Mr. Holmes, I do not know whether to thank you from the bottom of my heart or to curse your name for evermore for your part in exposing my crime. Yes, I did it, and I am glad that he is gone out of my life and the lives of all the other women he has tormented. I regret taking his life, though. I cannot say that I did it deliberately, and I cannot say that it was an accident. I am sorry for poor Olivia, and I am sorry for Mrs. Godney. I hope that she will thank me for removing Lionel from her life. I hope... I do not know what I hope..."

With that, she broke into a fit of sobbing as the constable led her away.

" Well," said Braithwaite as the door closed. " How did you come by all that, Mr. Holmes ? I was in the same room as you, I saw and heard all that you saw and heard, and yet I was in the dark, while you were shining light all around. How did Godney come to die, for example ?"

" Watson will confirm that the injection of air into the bloodstream will cause a painful and rapid death. When she stabbed at him with the empty syringe, the plunger was depressed. By bad luck she must have hit a blood vessel, and the air bubble entered his bloodstream."

" So it was an accident ?"

" You could make out to be such, certainly. My first clue that a third party was involved came when I noted the scent of rose water. Whence had that come ? It must have been from a person who did not work at the hospital. Sister Lightfoot informed us of the identity of that person. The fact that Miss de Lacey had obviously suffered from opiate poisoning, and Godney had not done so posed a slight problem, but that was resolved when I examined the syringe and formed the hypothesis regarding his death that I just described to you."

" How did you know that the syringe had been used to inject the laudanum into the chocolates and then cleaned and left to dry ?"

" A bow drawn at a venture. It proved to hit the target, I think."

" Where did the photograph of the prisoner and the murdered man come from ?"

" Ah, there you must forgive me. I abstracted it from his desk drawer while you and Watson were otherwise occupied. I had a fair idea of what I was looking for, after Sister Lightfoot had told us about Captain Cardew and his wife. But the really damning evidence came with the open bodice. It was meant to appear that it had been ripped open, when in fact it had been opened with a little care. And then our fair criminal over-gilded the lily."

" The buttons ?"

" Precisely. Cutting them rather than tearing them off was a careless error, but it was ridiculous for her to imagine that had he indeed ripped them from their place, Godney would still be holding them in his hand. The art of the criminal, like that of the painter, consists of knowing when to stop."

" I thank you most sincerely, Mr. Holmes," said Braithwaite at the end of this recital. He rose and shook hands with Holmes. " I am more than grateful to you for your assistance."

" All the credit shall be yours, Inspector," Holmes told him. " I do not wish my name to be mentioned in connection with this case."

" That is uncommonly generous of you, sir," said Braithwaite.

" Nonsense. Consider it my Christmas gift to you. It is, after all, the season of peace and goodwill, and God knows there is little enough of either at this time. Let me attempt to redress the balance in this small fashion. A very Happy Christmas to you, Inspector Braithwaite."

IF YOU ENJOYED THIS BOOK...

HANK you for reading these stories – I hope you enjoyed them.

It would be highly appreciated if you left a review or rating online somewhere.

You may also enjoy some of my other books, which are available from the usual outlets.

Acknowledgments

HERLOCK Holmes continues to fascinate many, long after his " death". I am delighted that so many people have expressed their satisfaction with my attempts to tell of his adventures, and I thank all of you who have encouraged me with your kind words, comments, and reviews.

I am also grateful to my wife Yoshiko, who has patiently endured my mental journeys to 19th-century London, and furthermore, has joined me on a more physical journey, moving our life halfway across the world, from Japan to the United Kingdom.

Special thanks are due to Jo, the late " Boss Bean" of Inknbeans Press, who supported me and helped me create more and better than I would ever manage unaided.

ALSO BY HUGH ASHTON

SHERLOCK HOLMES TITLES

More from the Deed Box of John H. Watson M.D.

Secrets from the Deed Box of John H. Watson M.D.

The Case of the Trepoff Murder

The Darlington Substitution

Notes from the Dispatch-Box of John H. Watson M.D.

Further Notes from the Dispatch-Box of John H. Watson M.D.

The Reigate Poisoning Case: Concluded

The Death of Cardinal Tosca

The Last Notes from the Dispatch-Box of John H. Watson M.D.

Without My Boswell

1894

Some Singular Cases of Mr. Sherlock Holmes

The Adventure of Vanaprastha

GENERAL TITLES

Tales of Old Japanese

The Untime

The Untime Revisited

Balance of Powers

Leo's Luck

Beneath Gray Skies

Red Wheels Turning

At the Sharpe End

Angels Unawares

TITLES FOR CHILDREN

Sherlock Ferret and the Missing Necklace

Sherlock Ferret and the Multiplying Masterpieces

Sherlock Ferret and the Poisoned Pond

Sherlock Ferret and the Phantom Photographer

ABOUT THE AUTHOR

UGH Ashton was born in the United Kingdom, and moved to Japan in 1988, where he lived until a return to the UK in 2016.

He is best known for his Sherlock Holmes stories, which have been hailed as some of the most authentic pastiches on the market, and have received favourable reviews from Sherlockians and non-Sherlockians alike.

He currently divides his time between the historic cities of Lichfield, and Kamakura, a little to the south of Yokohama, with his wife, Yoshiko.

Contact him through hashton@mac.com